THE END OF DAYS

Jenny Erpenbeck, consists ... the acclaimed ... , each leading to a different death of the same unnamed female protagonist. How could it all have gone ... intermezzos.

The first chapter begins with the death of a baby in the early twentieth-century Habsburg Empire. In the next chapter, the same girl grows up in Vienna after World War I, but a pact she makes with a young man leads to a second death. In the next scenario, she survives adolescence and moves to Russia with her husband. Both are dedicated Communists, yet our heroine ends up in a labor camp. But her fate does not end there ...

A novel of incredible breadth and amazing concision, and the winner of the prestigious Hans Fallada Prize, *The End of Days* offers a unique overview of the twentieth century by "one of the finest, most exciting auth... ..." (Michael Faber)

The End of Days

Also by Jenny Erpenbeck

FICTION

The Book of Words
The Old Child and Other Stories
Visitation

JENNY ERPENBECK

The End of Days

Translated by Susan Bernofsky

A NEW DIRECTIONS BOOK

The translation of this work was supported by a grant from the Goethe-Institut, which is funded by the German Ministry of Foreign Affairs.

First published in cloth by New Directions in 2014
Manufactured in the United States of America
New Directions Books are printed on acid-free paper.
Design by Erik Rieselbach

Library of Congress Cataloging-in-Publication Data
Erpenbeck, Jenny, 1967–
[Aller Tage abend. English]
The end of days / Jenny Erpenbeck ; translated from the German by Susan Bernofsky.
pages cm
ISBN 978-0-8112-2192-4 (alk. paper)
I. Bernofsky, Susan, translator. II. Title.
PT2665.R59A6413 2014
833'.92—dc23   2014014078

10 9 8 7 6 5 4 3 2 1

New Directions Books are published for James Laughlin
by New Directions Publishing Corporation
80 Eighth Avenue, New York 10011

We left from here for Marienbad only last summer.
And now—where will we be going now?

—W. G. SEBALD, *Austerlitz*

The End of Days

BOOK I

1

The Lord gave, and the Lord took away, her grandmother said to her at the edge of the grave. But that wasn't right, because the Lord had taken away much more than had been there to start with, and everything her child might have become was now lying there at the bottom of the pit, waiting to be covered up. Three handfuls of dirt, and the little girl running off to school with her satchel on her back now lay there in the ground, her satchel bouncing up and down as she runs ever farther; three handfuls of dirt, and the ten-year-old playing the piano with pale fingers lay there; three handfuls, and the adolescent girl whose bright coppery hair men turn to stare at as she passes was interred; three handfuls tossed down into the grave, and now even the grown woman who would have come to her aid when she herself had begun to move slowly, taking some task out of her hands with the words: oh, Mother— she too was slowly being suffocated by the dirt falling into her mouth. Beneath three handfuls of dirt, an old woman lay there in the grave: a woman who herself had begun to move slowly, one to whom another young woman, or a son, at times might have said: oh, Mother—now she, too, was waiting to have dirt thrown on top of her until eventually the grave would be full again, in fact even a bit fuller than full, since after all the mound of earth on a grave is always round on top because of the body underneath, even if the body lies far below the surface where no one can see. The body of an infant that has died unexpectedly produces hardly any roundness at all. But really the mound ought to be as huge as the Alps, she thinks, even though she's never seen the Alps with her own eyes.

She sits on the very same footstool she always used to sit on as a child when her grandmother was telling stories. This footstool was the one thing she asked for when her grandmother offered to give her something for her new home. She sits in the hallway on this footstool, leaning against the wall, her eyes closed, not touching the food and drink a friend has set before her. For seven days she will sit like this. Her husband tried to pull her to her feet, but he couldn't manage it against her will. When the door clicked shut behind him, she was glad. Just this past Friday, the infant's great-grandmother had stroked the sleeping child's head, calling her *meydele*, little girl. She herself, by giving birth to the child, had turned her grandmother into a great-grandmother and her mother into a grandmother, but now all these transformations have been reversed. The day before yesterday, her mother—who at the time could still be called a grandmother—had brought a woolen blanket for her to wrap herself in when she went walking in the park with her baby on cold days. Then, in the middle of the night, her husband had shouted at her to do something. But she hadn't known what to do in a situation like this. After his shouting, and after the few minutes in the middle of the night when she hadn't known what to do, after the moment when her husband, too, hadn't known what to do, he had not spoken another word to her. In her distress, she'd run to her mother (who now was no longer a grandmother), and her mother had told her to go back home and wait, she would send help. While her husband was pacing up and down the living room, she hadn't dared to touch her child again. She had carried all the buckets of water out of the house and emptied them, had draped a sheet over the hallway mirror, flung open the windows in the room where the child lay, to let the night in, and then sat down beside the cradle. With these gestures she had called to mind that part of life inhabited by human beings. But what had happened right here in her own home, not quite one hour before, was something no human hand could grasp.

That's just how it had been when her child was born, not even eight months before. After a night, a day, and another night during which the child hadn't arrived, she had wanted to die. That's how far she had withdrawn from life during those hours: from her husband, who was waiting outside; from her mother, who sat on a chair in the corner of the room; from the midwife, who was fussing about with bowls of water and towels; and above all, from this child that supposedly was there inside her but had wedged itself into invisibility. In the morning, after the birth, she watched from her bed as everyone simply went about doing what was needed: Her mother, who had now been transformed into a grandmother, received a friend arriving to offer congratulations, and her grandmother, now transformed into a great-grandmother, brought amulets printed with Psalm 21 to hang around the room and a cake fresh from the oven, and her husband had gone to the inn to drink the child's health. She herself was holding the baby in her arms, and the baby was wearing the linens that she, her mother and her grandmother had embroidered in the months preceding the birth.

There were even rules for what was happening now. The people her mother had sent arrived at dawn, took the baby from its cradle, wrapped it in a cloth, and laid it on a large bier. The bundle was so small and light that one of them had to hold it in place as they descended the stairs, otherwise it would have rolled off. *Zay moykhl un fal mir mayne trep nit arunter*. Do me a favor, don't go falling down the stairs. A favor. She knew the baby had to be buried before the day was out.

7

★

Now she sits here on this little wooden footstool that her grandmother gave her on her wedding day, she sits with her eyes closed, just as she has seen others sitting in times of mourning. Sometimes it was she who brought food to mourners; now a girlfriend has set bowls of food at her feet. Just as she emptied out all the water in the house the night before—they say the Angel of Death would wash his sword in it—just as she covered the mirrors and opened the window because she'd seen others do so before her (but also so the child's soul wouldn't turn back, so it would fly off forever)—in just this way she will now sit here for seven days: because she has seen others sitting like this, but also because she wouldn't know where else to go while she is refusing to enter that inhuman place her child's room became last night. The customs of man are like footholds carved into inhumanity, she thinks, something a person who's been shipwrecked can clutch at to pull himself up, and nothing more. How much better it would be, she thinks, if the world were ruled by chance and not a God.

Maybe the blanket was too thick, that could have been the cause. Or because the baby was sleeping on its back. Maybe it choked. Or it was sick and no one knew. Or the reason was that you could hardly hear the baby crying through the closed doors. She hears her mother's footsteps in the baby's room and knows what she is doing: She is taking the blankets out of the cradle and pulling off the pillowcases, she is stripping the cradle's fabric canopy from its wooden frame and pushing the cradle into a corner. With an armful of bed linens, she now emerges from the room, passing the footstool where her daughter is sitting with her eyes shut, and carries everything down to the laundry. Was it that she'd been too young to know what to do? Her mother never told her about all these things. Or because her husband was equally helpless. Because in truth she had been left all on her own with this child, this creature

8

that had to be kept alive. Because no one had told her beforehand that life does not work like a machine. Her mother comes back. As she walks past, she removes the sheet covering the hall mirror, folds it up, and carries it into the baby's room. She lays it at the bottom of the suitcase she's brought along for just this purpose, then takes the child's things from their drawer and puts them in the suitcase with the sheet. During the months that preceded the child's birth, all of them—the pregnant woman, her mother, and her grandmother—sewed, knitted and embroidered these jackets, dresses, and caps. Her mother now shuts the empty drawer. On top of the chest is the toy with little silver bells. When she picks it up, the bells make a jingling sound. They jingled yesterday as well, when her daughter was still a mother playing with her child. The jingling hasn't changed in the twenty-four hours that have passed since then. Her mother now places the toy on top of everything else in the suitcase, shutting it and picking it up before exiting the room and carrying it down the hall past her daughter to bring it to the cellar. Maybe it was because the child hadn't yet been baptized and its parents had married in haste with only a civil ceremony. Today, the child was buried in accordance with Jewish custom, and in accordance with Jewish custom she will now sit for seven days upon this footstool; but her husband will not speak to her. Surely he's now at church, praying for the soul of their child. And where can their child's soul go now? To purgatory? Paradise? Hell? Or was it—as some people say—that their child was one of those who needed only a short while to complete something begun in an earlier life, something of which the parents knew nothing, which is why the child so quickly returned to where it came from? Her mother comes back, goes into the baby's room and shuts the windows. Maybe on the other side of life there is nothing at all? The apartment is now perfectly still. In fact, that's what she would prefer.

Around nightfall, her breasts begin to grow hard and ache. She still has milk—milk for a baby lying in the ground. She'd like best to die now of this overabundance. When her baby was still gasping for air and then turning blue, she had imagined making the child a gift of all the years of life still remaining to her, haggling with the God of her forefathers, exchanging her own life for the life that had emerged from her. But God, if he existed, had rejected her gift. She remained alive. Now she remembers once more how after her marriage her grandmother never again permitted her to come along on visits to her grandfather. Only after her baby arrived and she insisted on showing it to him did she learn that on her wedding day her grandfather had sat shiva for her, his granddaughter, the living bride who had married a goy; despite his weakness he had sat there on his bed for seven days. From above, seen from the heaven her grandfather believes in, she too has already crossed the border from life to death and no longer possesses anything she might barter to strike a deal with God. When night comes, she pushes aside the bowls of food and lies down to sleep beside the footstool. She doesn't hear her mother go to bed. She doesn't even hear her husband come home. Sometime during this night it is exactly twenty-four hours since the unexpected death, in a small Galician town—50.08333 degrees latitude north, 25.15000 degrees longitude east—of an infant child.

2

An old man lies in bed in a dark cottage and does not speak. He's been lying like this for a long time now, day in and day out, he knows people are saying he's on his deathbed, but while for some people dying is a narrow antechamber to be crossed in a single leap or stride, the dying in which he lies is so huge that he cannot find his way across, perhaps because he is already so weak.

His wife sits beside him, she sits for a long time without saying anything; meanwhile it's already dark again outside. The Lord gave, and the Lord took away, she says at last.

That spring his wife had often sat knitting beside him, and although his eyes were no longer so good, he had seen that the garments she was working on were very small. And then one day she had taken the provisions that were to have lasted an entire week, baked a cake and left the house with it. There was no egg in the soup on the Sabbath. There was no need for him to ask, nor for her to explain.

Early this morning while it was still dark, still half asleep, he heard his wife and daughter whispering in the parlor; then, after lunch, his wife left the house and didn't return until nightfall, sitting down beside him and saying at last after a long silence: The Lord gave, and the Lord took away.

The old couple hadn't been invited to their granddaughter's wedding. On the day their granddaughter married a goy, the old man sat up in his bed and stayed sitting like that for seven days, sitting shiva for this living bride as was customarily done only for the dead.

Now his wife sits in silence beside him, her elderly, bed-ridden husband, and shakes her head. God knows what our *meydele* was thinking, marrying her daughter to a goy, the old man says.

3

She takes the blankets out of the cradle, takes off the pillowcases, strips the cradle's fabric canopy from its wooden frame, and pushes the cradle into a corner. The misfortune had begun many years before, when her daughter was still an infant. When they heard the noise outside, her husband had immediately sent the wet nurse up to the nursery with the baby, telling her to bolt the door and not open it under any circumstances if there was a knock, and to close the shutters tightly. Then the two of them ran from window to window downstairs to see what was going on: A crowd appeared to be forming in the surrounding streets, and across the way, on the square, some were running, some were shouting, but what they were shouting was unclear. She and her husband hadn't managed to get the downstairs shutters closed before the first stones struck the house. Her husband tried to see who was throwing the stones and recognized Andrei. Andrei, he shouted out the window, Andrei! But Andrei didn't hear him—or pretended not to, which was more likely, since he knew perfectly well who lived in the house he was throwing stones at. Then one of Andrei's stones came hurtling through a window pane, passing just a hair's breadth from her head, and crashed into the glass-fronted bookcase behind her, striking Volume 9 of the leather-bound edition of Goethe's *Collected Works* that her husband's parents had given him as a gift when he finished school. *No breath of air disturbs the place, / Deathly silence far and wide. / O'er the ghastly deeps no single / Wavelet ripples on the tide.* Hereupon her husband, filled with rage, flung open the front door, apparently intending to seize Andrei by the collar and bring him to his senses, but when he saw Andrei running toward the house with three or four other young men, one of them brandishing an axe, he slammed it shut again at once. Quickly, he turned the key in the lock, and together with his wife tried to take up the boards that always stood ready beside the door, waiting for just such an emergency, taking them and trying to nail them over the door. But it was already too late for this—where were the nails, where the hammer?—for the door was already beginning to splinter beneath the blows of the axe. Andrei, Andrei. Then she and her husband ran up the stairs, banging on the door behind which the wet nurse sat with the baby, but she didn't open the door: either because she didn't understand who was asking to be let in, or because she was so frightened she was unwilling to open it. The woman and her husband then fled to the attic, up one last steep flight of stairs, while down below, Andrei and his men were already bursting into the house. On the ground floor, the intruders smashed the remaining window panes, ripped the window frames from the wall, knocked down the bookcase, sliced open the eiderdowns, smashed plates and jars of preserves, threw the contents of the pantry out into the street, but then one of them must have heard her and her husband trying to lock the attic door, for without stopping on the second floor, the men now raced up the stairs, tearing down the wallpaper as they ran and banging holes in the wall with the axe. She and her husband stood behind the attic door, which was very thin, they'd locked it but hadn't found furniture heavy enough to barricade the door, and now they heard the men's footsteps on the last steep flight of stairs. *Hear my prayer, O Lord, and give ear unto my cry; hold not thy peace at my tears: for I am a stranger with thee, and a sojourner, as all my fathers were. O spare me, that I may recover strength, before I go hence, and be no more.* O Lord in heaven. If the way below was barred to them, there had to be an escape route above. They began to push the roof shingles away with their hands, creating an opening. But the door behind them that was momentarily holding off their pursuers was thin, just a few boards. Her husband helped her pull herself up and clamber through the opening onto the roof. And then she tried to pull him up after her. And that's when the thin door could no longer withstand the attackers' blows. And then she was pulling him up by one arm while the men below were pulling him down by the other. Lot refused to surrender the angels who were his guests. Lot stood on the threshold, and the mob seized him by the arm, trying to pull him out into the street to be punished for the hospitality he extended, wanting to have at least *him* to strike at, spit on, trample, and abuse; but the angels took hold of his other arm from inside the house with their angelic hands, and they were strong, they smote his attackers with blindness, pulled Lot back into the house, shut the door between him and the people, and those outside could no longer see one another, could no longer even see the door to Lot's house, they groped their way along the walls and had no choice but to withdraw. *Make no tarrying, O my God.* She doesn't have the strength of angels, she doesn't succeed in pulling her husband up to where she is. As she holds tight to her husband's arm, she implores Andrei, whom she has known since he was a baby, to have mercy, and she implores the men she doesn't know to have mercy as well, including the one holding the axe, but while she is still holding tight to her husband's hand, her husband down below is being first insulted and then beaten by the men she doesn't know and also by Andrei, whom she has known since he was a baby, Mercy, and finally before her eyes they begin to swing the axe. She does not let go. First she is holding her husband by the hand, and then all she is holding is a clump of flesh, for there is no longer anything alive left that she might pull up to where she crouches in the open air. Then she is a Jewish widow holding Death by the hand. She lets go, gets up, and looks down at the small town beneath her and the open landscape. It's broad daylight, there are thatch roofs and roofs covered in shingles, there are streets, squares, and fountains, and in the distance fields and woods, cows standing in a meadow, a coach driving down a dirt road, in front of the house people stand looking up at her, unmoving now and silent. Then, suddenly, she sees that it is snowing. Everything will freeze, she thinks, and a good thing too, she thinks, snow, snow. Losing consciousness, she tumbles, rolls down off the sloping roof, and falls, as luck would have it, on the heap of clothes, linens, and curtains thrown out onto the street by the men, and she remains lying there in the heap of rags, amid blood consisting of the raspberry jam she herself made the summer before, the jar shattered when it was thrown, and now she lies there, her limbs broken, her eyes closed, and none of the people standing there silently in the square comes closer or checks to see if she is still alive. She is alive, but at this moment she herself does not yet know it. The flurries have been further stirred up by her fall, more feathers float into the air from the slashed comforters, delicate goose down drifts around, slowly descending upon the branches of the trees: snow, snow, just like in winter.

With an armful of linens she now leaves the baby's room and walks past the footstool where her daughter is sitting. It was no accident that she married her daughter to a Christian. When her daughter was old enough to ask questions, she told her that her father had just gone off one day and never returned. Why did he leave? Where did he go? Will he come back again some day?

New panes of glass were set into the bookcase. She sold the house in the ghetto and moved to the center of town, where she took over her husband's business and set aside everything she could spare for her daughter's dowry. For many years now she has known something that her daughter will soon be forced to learn: A day on which a life comes to an end is still far from being the end of days.

4

So now something he has suspected his entire life, especially these past three years, has become glaringly obvious: If you get even the slightest bit off track, the consequences in the end are just as inescapable as if you'd gone and leapt headfirst into this or that abyss. As an Imperial and Royal civil servant responsible for a thirty-five-kilometer stretch of the Galician Railway of Archduke Karl Ludwig, he knew that everything depended on his ability not only to produce order, but to maintain it where it already existed. But in his own life, life had always intervened. During the year he spent as a trainee not yet receiving a salary, his hunger had caused him to incur debts. So by the time the year ended and he assumed his post as a regular civil servant of the eleventh—i.e. lowest—pay-grade, he was already deep in debt. His hunger, to be sure, was a sign he was still alive, as was his freezing during that first winter—but now his debts would count as a demerit when he underwent his Confidential Qualification, an evaluation carried out behind closed doors by his superiors. Thus, it was impossible to say when he would be promoted from the eleventh to the tenth pay-grade and be able to start paying back what he owed; no one would discuss this with him. In short, he had no prospect of making the leap back to ordinary life. Hunger and freezing guaranteed more hunger and freezing, that's how it was when life got the upper hand even once. Then he'd met the Jewish shopkeeper and her daughter, whose skin was so white it would have blinded him like snow if he'd been a bug crawling around on it. If only he'd been able to see where the track was and where it wasn't when he proposed to her. There's no paying down debts with a Jewish dowry, even if you pay them down. And there are differences. You can recognize them by the silence surrounding you at the clubhouse or the office. This silence has to do with consequences, with the end in general—he's come to understand this, having finally grasped it now that the end is staring him in the face. Why was the baby so quiet all of a sudden?

His father hadn't come when they got married at the civil registry office, nor for the birth of their child. He said the trip was too long and too expensive. It had been three years since he'd seen him last, and if all went well, he might never have to see him again. The morning after the child's birth, he'd gone to an inn alone and toasted the newborn with strangers, and while he was swirling the schnapps around in his mouth with his tongue before swallowing it, savoring the taste, it occurred to him that his tiny daughter also had a tongue in her mouth, she'd come equipped with her own insides when she slipped out of her mother, emerging from her mother's concavity with concavities of her own. He, the civil servant, eleventh class, had begotten a living thing, and no Confidential Qualification was required to verify this fact.

Two hundredweights of twine are required to adorn the Brody station with flowers in honor of the Kaiser, whose train will be passing through. Thick oak planks fifteen centimeters across to replace the ties between the tracks. Six hundred gulden a year is the salary of a civil servant eleventh class, while a civil servant tenth class receives eight hundred and if he's lucky another two hundred as a bonus. But what to do with all the things that resisted calculation? How much time was there really between the second when a child was alive and the next, when it was no longer alive? Was it even time separating one such moment from another? Or did it have to be given a different name, except that no one had found the right name for it yet? How could you calculate the force dragging a child over to the realm of the dead?

He can still remember the moment when he imagined for the first time what the white cleft between his bride's legs must look like, fleshy and firm, and when he spread it apart with his fingers, the tiny red rooster's comb would appear. Later, when she was his wife, he loved the sounds their two sweaty bodies made when they rubbed together and pulled apart again, slapping and smacking, their mouths, tongues, and lips all flowing together, sucking at one another to transform two formerly separate beings into a single moist concavity of flesh. Flesh, flesh—sometimes the word alone was enough to arouse him. But ever since the night before, when he took the lifeless child from his wife's arms and laid it back in its cradle, he knows how cold something dead feels, colder than he would have ever expected. He doesn't know how he can forget this. He, the civil servant, eleventh class, has begotten something dead, and no Confidential Qualification is needed to confirm this.

Sunlight falls on the rough pine floor of the inn where he is sitting.... When he arrived before dawn, there were still a couple of Russian deserters lying under the tables asleep. While he was downing his first glass of spirits, and then the second, and the third, they woke up, gathered their bundles, and left in the company of a short, bald-headed man who'd appeared at daybreak, apparently by prearrangement. Neither the bald-headed man nor the others spoke much, nonetheless it was clear that these Russians—a sort you often saw in public houses like this—were men who'd made up their minds not to turn back. . . . After his experience of the night before, the civil servant, eleventh class, finds himself suddenly understanding what it means to cross a border like that, what it means to no longer have any possibility of retreat. It's as if the top layer were crumbling away from everything he sees and encounters, this layer that had previously gotten in the way of his comprehension, and now, like it or not, he is forced to recognize what lies below and to endure this recognition—but he can't imagine how.

Sometimes, looking at his baby, he had wondered where it came from, where it had been before its mother conceived it. Now he wishes it made no difference whether the child had appeared—remaining only for the most infinitesimally fleeting bit of time—or had never appeared at all. But no, there was a difference. Using his thumb, he rubs a shiny coat button shiny. Since there was no measurement that applied to the difference between life and death, the dying of this tiny child was as absolute as any other dying. Never before has measuring—his profession, after all—seemed so superfluous to him as on that morning. Should he pull everyday life back on over his head now that he has understood it is nothing more than a garment?

He'd shouted at his wife because—although she'd picked up the baby, trying to comfort it—she hadn't known what to do, hadn't known any remedy for death, but he had also shouted because he too had known no remedy for death.

He, the civil servant of the lowest possible class, had been no match for Death.

And now?

The short, bald-headed man returns to the pub, sits at a table near the Imperial and Royal civil servant he'd seen there earlier that morning when he came for the Russians, and nods. The civil servant had carelessly tossed his coat with the gold buttons over an empty chair; if it were not for this coat, the bald-headed man wouldn't have known that this person he saw sitting here ought to have been sitting in an office by this hour. The civil servant is unshaven, the tips of his mustache soiled, he is wearing no necktie, and there is a full glass of spirits before him yet again as he gazes out the window at the street, where some mongrel is running in circles trying to catch its own tail, occasionally sliding on a frozen puddle, the mongrel stumbles around before finding its footing and then goes back to hunting down its own scruffy posterior. The bald man orders a snack—pickled herring along with a beer—and settles down contentedly. He isn't ruling out the possibility of striking yet another deal here this very morning.

5

It's true, she is awake, and now there is this next day, and this day, too, she will spend sitting on the footstool. During the night or early that morning, her mother apparently cleared away the bowls of food, untouched by the mourner. She hears someone clattering around in the kitchen, water splashing, something being pushed aside on the table, footsteps crossing the floor, the clink of porcelain. In the baby's room, in any case, there is nothing left to do. It wasn't as she had feared yesterday: that while she was sleeping she would forget what had happened and the memory would come crashing down on her with all its weight when she woke up. No, all through her sleep she had known that her child was no longer alive, and when she woke up, she knew it still, sleep had been no more and no less leaden than wakefulness, so she had been spared seeing her worn-out workaday reality collapse once more. When she rises to sit again upon the footstool, everything goes quiet in the kitchen, as if her mother is listening to see what she is up to now that she's stirring again. Why has life at home become so much like hunting? In the parlor, the miniature grandfather clock strikes six with bright, tinny strokes, then all is perfectly quiet once more. Her husband, it would appear, is still out. Yesterday, when they returned to the house after the funeral and she sat down on the stool, he had tried to lift her up, and when he didn't succeed, he ran out of the house. She hasn't seen him since. Will the same thing now happen to her as happened to her mother? When, as a little girl, she tried to imagine where her father might be instead of with his family, she always envisioned someone who had hanged himself. Father might be in America, her mother had said. Or in France. But she didn't believe it. Her mother always spoke of her father's absence as something definitive, irreversible, never allowing her daughter the faintest hope that he might return home, or even prove to be nearby—in the district capital, for instance, with another wife and new children. Sometimes, introducing herself, she had the impression people were caught off guard when she said her name. In America, her mother said, or in France. But she herself never imagined her father as a living man, neither in America nor France, nor saw him living nearby; she only ever envisioned him as someone who had, for instance, hanged himself; and if anything was nearby, it was the forest where his body had swung, maybe she'd already walked right past the tree he'd tied his noose to.

Do you need anything, her mother asks. Behind her, the sun is shining into the kitchen, which is why her mother looks like a silhouette. The daughter shakes her head. On this second day of sitting, she and her mother don't say much. No one knows her mother better than she does, and no one knows her better than her mother, so there's not much to say. She sits there, thinking about the fact that a part of her is now lying in the ground and beginning to rot, then she looks at her skin, which is still surrounded by air, alive. A friend comes to visit, she has more bowls with her, and says: You'll have a second child, and a third and a fourth. She says: We'll see. One of the bowls her friend has brought has eggs in it, she knows this is customary, but doesn't want to eat them. One neighbor doesn't even knock, she just bursts in, violently weeping, and doesn't even scrape the snow from her shoes before falling along with her tears at the mourner's feet, Praised be our sole Judge, she cries, and then gets up again to fling her arms around the neck of the mourner's mother, sobbing, why oh why, shaking her head, and then she stops saying anything at all because she is weeping so hard her voice is not available for use. Simon, the coachman, comes, he stops just inside the hallway door and says he's sorry and that he's brought a bit of soup and that his wife sends her condolences, unfortunately she can't come herself because she's so sick. Another of her friends comes and says: Right from the beginning I thought it was pale. Then another: Why didn't you send for the doctor? Did it really happen that fast? A third: When they're so young, the slightest little thing is enough to do them in, who knows what the Lord in His infinite greatness was thinking! A fourth: Where in the world is your husband?

In the evening her grandmother arrives, sits down on the floor beside her, takes her stocking feet in her lap and warms them with her hands, only then is the granddaughter able to cry for the first time since the death of her child. On the third day this, that, and the other visitor comes. As if approaching an altar, friends and former neighbors from the ghetto come to stand before the footstool with its mourner, bringing her food and words of comfort, they themselves know what it means to lose a child, or else they don't know, and no doubt quite a few of them are pleased that it happened to be the one who married the goy, etc., but that's not what they say, instead they say, for example: But of course the main thing is that you yourself are still alive. As for her, she is incapable of crying when visitors are there, and by the third day she is very weary of being the recipient of all the comfort and support it is the sacred duty of these visitors to bestow on her, she doesn't know how she can bear it that her child's death still persists, that from now on it will persist for all eternity and never diminish, but she doesn't speak of this to anyone. On the evening of the third day she knows that if her husband has not yet returned, he is not going to. She asks her mother what it is like to live without a husband. Her mother says: Hard. One of her friends says: You'll see, tomorrow at the latest he'll be back, he's probably just drowning his sorrows. Her grandmother sits down beside her and sings her a lullaby. Has the time in which she was a grown woman now come to an end? If she has missed the road leading forward, will time simply reverse itself and go back again? On the fourth day, her own mourning seems alien to her and she thinks that perhaps it doesn't really matter whether a being is on one side of the border or the other. On the fifth day, her mother says, we have to think about what comes next. On the sixth day, the clock strikes all the hours contained in a day, with its bright, tinny chime. Might it be time now to go looking for her father, if he happens not to have hanged himself? On the morning of the seventh day, her mother helps her to get up and leads her to the table in the kitchen. Only after the daughter has sat down does her mother say to her: We have to start economizing. On this seventh day the daughter realizes for the first time that she herself is also a daughter, one who has been alive all this time and whose life is only now, with a short delay of seventeen years, breaking down. No one can predict when it will be revealed that a wish is going to be left unfulfilled. Her mother sits down beside her, takes her hands, and says: Your father was beaten to death by the Poles.

6

Now he knows where to find the agency, the bald-headed man gave him the address. When he goes out onto the street, it suddenly occurs to him that the first child of one of his colleagues also died young. One day, shortly after the baby's death, his colleague asked him if he wanted to see the grave. Yes, he said, although he didn't really want to, and so the two of them walked across the cemetery during their lunch break. His colleague showed him the child's name on an iron plaque on a wall to the left, the mound of earth in front of it, and the stone border with the little railing. Not even a year and a half later, this same colleague became a father again, and the newborn was given the name of the deceased child as its middle name when it was baptized. He goes into the bank to withdraw the sum his journey will cost. At the exchange office next door, he obtains the twenty dollars in American currency he'll need to enter the country, as the bald-headed man instructed him. He remembers how his wife laughed when he would imitate for her what she looked like when she was sleeping. They laughed at the same jokes over and over, laughing again and again at next to nothing; when his mother-in-law was with them, she rarely understood what they were going on about and would just shrug. Soon his train will pass over the very rails he looked after until now, one hour and twenty minutes is what this leg of the journey will take, that's all—the stretch of track for which he used to be responsible is tiny compared to the length of the entire journey he now intends to embark on. When he embraced his wife, her bosom fit perfectly below the curve of his ribs. Sometimes they would just stand there like that, happy; sometimes they would make faces together in the mirror; once he had stuck the tip of his mustache in her ear; another time, rubbed his nose against hers.... The journey will take him by land to Bremen, and there, the bald-headed man explained to him, he will board a ship; the ship is called *Speranza*.... Then they asked themselves whether other people also did things like that when they were alone.

On his way to the station he sees his apartment building on the other side of the street and briefly stops. Something is taking place there that used to be called his life, all he has to do is cross the street and go upstairs, and he will be back where he belongs: beside his wife. Even from where he is standing he can hear the shrieks and wails coming from inside. Not his wife's voice—that much is certain—and if he's not mistaken, not the voice of his mother-in-law either. Who is shedding tears over his child? The door opens, and a woman he doesn't know comes out of the house in low-heeled shoes, her coat buttoned all the way up, her scarf covering her hair; as she walks, she wipes her tears, she hasn't noticed him on the other side of the street, and even if she did, she'd have no idea why he was standing there, and by the time she reaches the next corner, it won't even be possible to tell that she's been crying. When she turns off the street, an old man is coming from the other direction and almost bumps into her, he is holding a bowl. The old man nods to the woman, then continues slowly on his way to the building's front door, which he pushes open with his shoulder so that the contents of his bowl—perhaps soup that he wants to bring to the woman in mourning—will not spill. He, the highest ranking mourner, standing a stone's throw away, sees the stooped shoulders of the old man, and knows who it is: Simon, the coachman from the Jewish quarter who is usually off carting wood shavings, rubbish, and milk, he's often seen him from behind sitting atop his coach box. All the people here seem to know what their duty is, he's the only one asking himself what to do. If his mother were still alive, she would be praying the rosary with him now, he would be sitting beside the tiny coffin in the parlor and would be the father of the dead child. Is it a sign of cowardice if one leaves one's life behind, or a sign of character if one has the strength to start anew?

The question of whether the nursery should remain sealed up for-ever is one she doesn't have to answer, since it's obvious she must give up the entire apartment. The only option that remains to her is moving back in with her mother. Hadn't it pleased her when her husband married her—a Jew—without his parents' consent, and above all that his passion for her was so strong it made him forget his own origins? This time, she's the one he's taken a mind to aban-don, he is leaving her behind without her consent. She knows that his absence will be no greater and no smaller than his love for her and their child—and what she's seeing reflected now in the line of death is in the end nothing more than the bond joining him to her.

You mustn't forget, child, that he used you to pay his debts.

That's not the only use I was to him: For example, I got in the way of his professional advancement. He would have spent all eter-nity in the eleventh pay grade for my sake.

But it wasn't all eternity.

That's because of the baby.

That's what you think. It just didn't occur to him beforehand that he hadn't done himself any favors by marrying you.

Is that supposed to console me?

Yes.

So now you also want to rob me of the days when I was happy.

I'm just saying: You never had as much as you imagine you're losing now.

Do you think I'd feel better if I saw things that way?

That's what I'm hoping.

So then I'd just put on my apron again and remind myself how much a herring weighs compared to three apples.

At least with herring and apples you know where you stand.

It's obviously been a long time since you loved someone.

That's unfair and you know it.

I don't want to talk anymore.

She'd always thought that when two people were united, it was a matter of crossing over a border you didn't cross with anyone else, of leaving the world behind and from then on sharing everything. Now she sees that this border is malleable and can shift about at times like this. Imperceptibly, the border has slid inward, and now it is once more separating him from her. Before, she was his freedom; now he's begun to seek his freedom elsewhere.

8

If only he knew where he could find death; he's hoping for an easy one now that he's been lying here so long waiting for it. *As light as a kiss. As easy as plucking a hair out of the milk.* A neighbor woman told him, without his asking, that the infant suffocated. Suffocation, it says in the Talmud, is the hardest among the 903 deaths. *Suffocation is like a briar that has gotten caught in wool, you tear it out with all your strength and throw it over your shoulder. Like a thick rope pulled through an opening that is too small.*

Whoso findeth, his friend congratulated him at his wedding fifty-two years before, and this finding continues today—find: the wisdom in the Torah, a good wife, a peaceful life, down to the last shovelful of earth on the coffin; find: a death easy as a kiss, *like the kiss with which the Lord awoke Adam to life*, he blew breath into his nose, and one day, if you're lucky, he'll gently, lightly kiss it away again. Finding is also what you need to do, he thinks, grinning his toothless graybeard grin, when you have an urgent need for the privy. I've got to go, he shouts into the next room, for without the help of his wife—who was his bride the day his friend wished him good fortune using the word *findeth* fifty-two years before—without her help, he can no longer get up.

26

Gray is the water—gray—and he throws up, why is it throwing when you throw up, he thinks, raising his head briefly, but then he's sick to his stomach again, he's never felt nausea like this in all his life. Once his wife told him that as a child she had long been convinced the world was as flat as a *palatschinke*, and she herself—like all the other inhabitants of the border town she lived in—had been sprinkled on the outermost rim of this pancake like a grain of sugar. When she lost her way on the outskirts of town, her one fear was that she might come too close to the border and suddenly fall off the edge. *My little grain of sugar.* And all the while, as she later learned at school, her horizon was nothing more than an imaginary line extending clear to the other side of Russia. As long as one remained in a single spot, this was genuinely difficult to understand, even for him, the young civil servant for whom the railway—meaning the locomotion of human beings—was a matter of professional concern. It's really only here, on this swaying ship, that he is truly internalizing what it means for the Earth to be a sphere. Not only is he made dizzy by its roundness as he circles it, unable to endure this circling; at the same time, the horizon keeps retreating before him, in motion, retreating ever farther, as though the swaying ship were remaining fixed in place to defy him, keeping him, the traveler, always the same distance from his destination, as though the journey's end were running away from him as he himself runs away, each canceling the other out as he continues to move. The water is gray, and he is overcome with nausea, just as sick to his stomach as several others standing there beside him, throwing up as well. The wind is blowing from the direction in which the ship is sailing, it tugs at the tails of his Imperial and Royal coat, chilling the spine of this man who until recently was a civil servant with a lifetime appointment, who meanwhile, bent over the back railing, is bequeathing to his native land in farewell everything with which it nourished him. After two or three days the nausea will let up, someone says behind him, it's the gentleman with whom he is sharing his second-class cabin, a Swiss gentleman who is just taking a stroll across the deck and, seeing his need, gives him a handkerchief, assuring him that after this initial period things will improve. The gentleman is apparently accustomed to traveling, he lets the wind tousle his shock of hair and now pulls out an apple, saying that on the contrary, the fresh air whets his appetite, he takes a bite and offers the young man an apple too, no thank you, the man says, turning to face the sea once more, I understand, says the bearer of apples, and tosses the second round thing down from the gallery to the travelers of the lowest class in the cargo hold, who surely are hungry but lack access to a railing of their own where they might throw up when nausea overtakes them.

10

And her? For approximately three years she weighs herring and apples, hands bread, milk, and matches across the counter.

You can't keep staring people in the face like that.

There's nothing else to look at.

It isn't proper. Only children stare like that.

No one's complained.

Mrs. Gmora doesn't come as often now, or Mr. Veitel.

I see you're keeping track.

I wouldn't say that, but I do have a good sense of my customers.

And I don't.

You do fundamentally.

I don't have to do this.

Why are you always so quick to take offense?

I'm not offended, but if my help isn't wanted here I can go elsewhere.

Really, so where would you go?

Her daughter says nothing.

That's not how I meant it, you know that.

I don't know anything at all.

They used to get their eggs from Johanna Sawitzki, but meanwhile it turns out that Karel's eggs are fresher. The price of kerosene for lamps has fallen because it's hard to sell Galician petroleum as fast as it degrades after being brought to the surface. For herring and sour pickles purchased together, they give their customers a better price than Levi.

In all the time you stand around waiting for customers you might have mopped the floor. For example.

Sure.

Child, this is your shop too, you're a grown woman now.

It was never my choice.

So now it's my fault?

What was the point of learning all that Goethe by heart at school?

Be glad you got to go to school at all.

Now the lie the shopkeeper had always sold her daughter as the truth has come to life after all. Now her daughter has taken her place as the abandoned wife, while she herself has become what in truth she always was, if only in secret: a widow.

11

Mrs. Gmora doesn't come as often, or Mr. Veitel, that may well be. But now there's the officer who's taken to stopping in for matches every day at precisely the hour when her mother is off making her rounds of the farms for milk and eggs. He'll say, perhaps, that he likes how she's wearing her hair, and she'll ask him, perhaps, if they use real bullets for their maneuvers. Or he'll say that it really ought not to rain when they're practicing their formations, and she'll say no one melts in a little rain and laugh, and he'll says it's pretty the way she laughs. And once, as she's handing him the matches across the counter, he suddenly pulls off his white leather glove before taking the matches and ever so briefly touches her hand, saying softly: I'm on fire, and she says: That'll be one groschen, the same as always, because she thinks she must have misheard. The next time, he says nothing at all and keeps his glove on, perhaps because her mother is standing right beside her, because on Sunday the farmers from whom she gets the eggs and milk are all at church. But then, at the beginning of the next week, when she is all alone behind the counter again, he wordlessly hands her a slip of paper along with the coin, gazing openly at her, and only after he is gone does she unfold the paper and read. All there is on the paper is: a street, a house number, a day, and a time. Aha, she thinks, and then she thinks that she wasn't mistaken after all. And later, in the evening, lying alone in her bed in which she lay as a little girl—the bed to which she returned after the death of her child so as to sleep herself old in it and, who knows, perhaps even die in it someday—later, in the evening, that hour of evening that might as well be night, she cannot think of a good reason not to go at the appointed hour to where the officer will be awaiting her.

Indeed, why not? Her husband is gone, she no longer has a child, and there's no need to tell her mother. She wants to go. When she thinks of the warm, dry, almost coarse hand of the officer, she feels almost dizzy with desire. Her desire branches out to the farthest reaches of her body, she is dizzy down into the joints of her fingers and toes, and between her legs. So this is what happens when temptation stops being just a word and enters into a life, when it slips beneath the skirt of a woman randomly chosen, seizing hold of her mortal body with terrible force. Exalted is the person who is tempted, for that person alone has the opportunity to resist, her grandfather explained to her years before, when, as an adolescent, she was sitting on the footstool and her mother had taken the horse and cart into the countryside to buy merchandise.

And what do you get for overcoming the temptation?

The resisting itself is the reward.

That means I'm paying myself.

Only if you resist.

If I resist.

The Lord wants you to demonstrate that you are worthy of him.

That's all He wants?

That's all He wants.

So really it's all about me.

All about you, as a part of the whole.

Then I myself am His test.

What do you mean?

If I don't resist, it means He didn't do his job well.

When her grandfather laughed, she could look inside his mouth and see how few teeth he had left.

It would most certainly be lamentable if He—who holds together the waters of the sea as if in a water skin—felt the need to test Himself using a slip of a thing like you.

But why else would He need my renunciation?

By then her legs were already so long that, crouching on the stool, she could effortlessly prop her chin on her knees. Because of her marriage to the goy, her grandfather sat shiva for her as though she had died. From then until his own death a year and a half ago, she never saw him again. Her grandfather disowned her, but even after this disowning, her life continued to go on and was still continuing today. What rules governed this life—this life that for him was no longer a life—was something she had no one to ask. From then on, her life was simply her life, that's all.

Once, they have to put on life jackets, because the ship is traveling through thick fog, and there's a risk of colliding with another ship; once it is storming so violently that an old woman tears the locket from the chain around her neck and throws it into the water with loud prayers, to reconcile God with the ship; once someone is heard playing the violin on one of the lower decks—a piece from the operetta *Die Fledermaus*—but the former civil servant doesn't recognize the music, even though he studied in Vienna. If he were to perish of the nausea that refuses to leave him, who would get his pocket watch and the coat with the gold buttons? The gentleman traveling with him shows a Polish child a banana and explains how such a thing is peeled. The gentleman bites off the little black tip of the banana himself and spits it into the sea. But the child doesn't want the banana. After two days, three, four, the young man's nausea still hasn't subsided. Only after an endlessly long twelve and a half days does he behold one morning, standing amid the throng suddenly crowding the deck, the Statue of Liberty, and this is definitely better than never having seen it. On their voyage, the gentleman told him of a German captain whose ship was so dilapidated that instead of venturing across the ocean with his passengers, he tacked up and down off the coast of Scotland, just far enough out that the land was out of sight. Nine days later he unloaded the emigrants in a small harbor, telling them that this was America. In both places, English was spoken, a language none of the new arrivals understood, and the men wore skirts, as was no doubt the latest fashion in New York—so it was nearly a week before the last of the emigrants understood that they were still in Europe. But by then the dilapidated captain had long since vanished along with the money they'd paid him for their passage to the New World.

Now, men, women, and children are weeping, overcome, they

keep pointing out the gigantic likeness of the woman to one another, some fling their arms around whoever happens to be standing close by; an elderly woman tries to embrace the Austrian, but he fends her off. All he'd done before he left was send his father a postcard. Why join the ranks of humankind now? Maybe he's just a cold person, he thinks for the first time ever, and wonders whether arriving in a foreign country is enough to turn one into a different man in the same skin. A child points to the statue and asks: Who's that? And he says: Columbus.

13

The building she's walking into looks no different from other buildings. It is Wednesday afternoon, the front door is still gleaming in the sun; she told her mother she was visiting a friend. She delayed her arrival by five minutes to be absolutely certain she wouldn't get there ahead of him. Before she lifts her hand to knock on the apartment door, he opens it, having heard her footsteps on the stairs. He draws her inside and immediately turns this drawing into an embrace, then the kiss, then she touches his teeth with her tongue, then she feels the corners of her mouth grow wet with his saliva, then she pushes him away, then he grasps her firmly, pressing the inside of his arm to her mouth, and she bites his arm because she doesn't know what else to do with it, and he says: Ah, she bites harder and he repeats: Ah, and she is seized with the desire to bite into him all the way to the bone; then he pushes her away, seizes her, and spins her around so he can open her dress, which is fastened up the back with a long row of hooks, and then her corset as well, meanwhile she bows her head to remove the pins from her hair, and this controlled, quiet activity is the preparation for something that—as has apparently been agreed—will be neither controlled nor quiet. The room he invited her to is small and furnished, the curtains yellowed, and the enamel is flaking off the wash basin sitting on a chest of drawers; but she sees none of this, instead she sees that the officer's close-fitting trousers display a noticeable bulge at the crotch, she runs her fingers across this bulge, feeling astonishment not only that this is allowed, but that she knows it is. A number of things are different this afternoon than they were with her husband, the officer's aroused member bends up rather than down, he licks her breasts, which her husband never did, and when she is lying on top of him, he slaps her buttocks resoundingly with his palm. Every single moment this afternoon is too late for her to leave again. But when the two hours he rented the room for are almost up, he kisses her cheek and says: Alas, my sweet, it's time to go. She watches him as he gets up, his legs are sinewy and long, far longer than those of her husband. He bends over to sort out their things—his and hers—that are lying in a heap on the floor, tossing the dress, corset, and stockings onto the bed for her and slipping into his close-fitting trousers. They no longer display a bulge. He doesn't know that she has already borne a child, and she would like to tell him so, but how? She too gets up and pulls on her stockings, meanwhile he is digging about in his wallet. Maybe she'll have another one after all, a child by him, she thinks and smiles. She slips into her corset, deftly hooking it shut. With or without a wedding—what does she care about that—now he's finally found the banknote he wants to give her—she'd be happy in any case. She pulls the dress on over her head, it rustles, and only when she has emerged again from the dress does she see the hand he is holding out to her with the money, his dry, warm hand that was the start of everything, she sees his hand with the banknote and almost wants to laugh, asking: What's the idea? But he doesn't laugh in return, instead he says, perhaps: For you. Or possibly something like: Don't make a fuss. Or: Keep the change. Or: You certainly earned it, my lovely. He says some sentence of this sort to her, and she looks at him as if seeing him for the first time.

He just nods to her and places the money on the chest of drawers, then spins her around with her back to him, as if she were a child that hasn't yet learned to get dressed on its own, he hooks her dress up the back as she stands there—seemingly immersed now in thoughts of her own—so that she can show herself on the street without attracting notice. As he leaves, he pulls on his white leather gloves and says:

Wait for a few minutes before you go down.

She neither looks at him nor responds, just stands there in the middle of the room, staring at the floor, staring as if the floor were opening to reveal an abyss he was unable to see.

14

When her husband—who despite his serious illness had lived longer than many healthy men—finally died, the old woman accepted her daughter's invitation, gave away all her chickens, packed up the Holy Scripture, the seven-armed candelabra, and her two sets of plates, and went to live with her. She left behind the semidarkness in which she'd been spending her life, along with a few pieces of furniture, their feet all scraped and scratched—her husband had taken a saw to them whenever they began to rot, shortening them by a centimeter or two—and left behind the dirt floor that was just the same as outside, her granddaughter had scratched letters into it with a stick when she was little. Soon the thatch roof would weigh down the now abandoned house, pressing it into the ground, and covering it until it decomposed.

Here in her daughter's apartment, all the rugs, tablecloths, and Chinese porcelain were sold long ago, after the goy ran off with her granddaughter's dowry, but her daughter has kept the apartment—

the floorboards are oak, worn to a shiny smoothness, the door handles are brass, and the light slants in through glass windows. Every morning the old woman walks through all the rooms with a goose feather, wiping away the dust gathering on the few pieces of furniture, then she takes her apron off and sits down on the sofa to read the Torah. *Turn it, and again turn it; for the all is therein, and thy all is therein: and swerve not therefrom, for thou canst have no greater excellency than this.* The only dowry she and her husband had been able to give her daughter when she married the prosperous merchant's son was their passion for the study of the Holy Books. For nights on end, the two young people, having put their daughter to bed, would sit up with her and her husband, debating whether the realm of God could truly be found here on Earth if one only knew how to look—whether, in other words, the riddle of life was concealed here in the human realm, or whether it existed only in the beyond. Whether as a matter of principle there were two different worlds or just the one. Only through a life spent in holiness, her husband said, could man succeed in uniting what had been sundered: the world to come and earthly life. But what was a life spent in holiness, his son-in-law asked, adding that all these matters depended on human interpretations of the Holy Scripture—which meant that a man's striving for the right life could be in error as well. Yes, her daughter had responded, you ought to be looking at everything mankind actually experiences on earth, it's not just a matter of what Holy Scripture says. The mother herself had believed in an eternal life existing on Earth, after all that's what she saw before her: She herself was there, and her old man, her daughter with her husband, and the tiny newborn girl that was sleeping soundly, her head thrust back. But after her daughter's husband had been beaten to death, there were no longer any conversations of this sort, her daughter had left the ghetto and when her own daughter was grown, she'd married her to a goy. Now the goy had gone off, her granddaughter was back to living with her mother as she had done in childhood, and when the mother wasn't there, the grandmother took care of her, just like before. A human life, then, was long enough to foil an escape plan.

When evening comes, the old woman sets aside her book, putting on her apron again. If there is meat, she begins her cooking by going down to the courtyard and cleaning her sharp knife by thrusting it into the ground, then pulling it out again, because in this household you can't count on anyone but her to respect the prescribed separation of dishes and implements. The kid may not be cooked in its mother's milk, that's all there is to it.

15

On Ellis Island, a tiny bit of land within eyeshot of Manhattan, the new arrivals are inspected to determine their suitability for a life of freedom. Their eyes are checked, their lungs, their throats, their hands, and finally their entire exposed bodies, men and women separately, children separately from their parents.

When they check your eyes, watch out for the man with the hook!

Why?

When he comes to check you, he can make your eye fall out.

No way.

It's true, a man told me about it, he said his eye fell right into his jacket pocket.

When it's his turn, he's brought into the examination room and told to undress completely. He doesn't understand the instructions in English, but even after an interpreter translates them for him, he doesn't move. Have the Americans lost their minds? Or do they really think of it as a second birth when you set foot in their country? In any case, his examinations at the Technical University in Vienna—which certainly weren't easy—had gone differently.

Come on, they say, meaning: Hurry up.

There's no help for it: More naked than he ever stood before his wife, he must now, like it or not, stand here in the light and present himself to an entire group of doctors. If only you could know in advance where the path you choose freely will lead. His coat and clothing are meanwhile being disinfected, when he gets them back after the examination they are crumpled. Shame, then, is the price one pays for this life of freedom, or is this itself the freedom: that shame no longer matters? Then America really must be Paradise.

16

Her husband has known for a year and a half what comes after death, and soon she will, too. Her daughter, on the other hand—although she's been a widow longer—has a good part of her path still before her. Keeping the shop is a struggle. What will become of her granddaughter when she is all alone in the world someday?

Two ships lie in the harbor. She holds her ears with their sagging lobes close to her husband's mouth—his whisper is so soft, she can scarcely hear the rest of the story, but she herself has read it often. *One of the two ships has just returned from a long voyage, the other is just preparing for a long voyage.* She tries to give her husband—for whom speaking is an exertion—something to drink, but he refuses to swallow, and so the water runs down his stubbly chin onto the pillow.

Jubilation and blessings accompany the ship as it sails off—while the arriving ship goes unremarked. But is it not this ship that deserves jubilation?

What a shame that she was able to raise only the one daughter with him. Two other children died shortly after birth. When on some evenings she wept over the ones that had died, he would sit down beside her with a nod.

The newly arrived ship lies safely in the harbor. But nothing is known of the one just setting sail. What will be its fate? Who knows whether it will successfully withstand the storms awaiting it?

Her daughter recently remarked that perhaps it would make more sense to close the store and rent out part of the apartment instead.

Or would you rather have some soup? she asks him.

The pillow is still damp with the water she tried to give him when he stops being able to breathe.

17

The shopkeeper can still clearly remember the day the goy first came into the shop and saw her daughter, who had just turned sixteen. Since he displayed serious interest, she summoned him not long afterward to have tea with her in their apartment while the girl was at school. She showed him the living room and the bookcase with Goethe's *Collected Works*, spoke of the dowry, and finally even brought him into her daughter's room, where the dress the girl had worn the day before was still draped over the back of the big armchair, one of the shoes beside it had fallen over, and the housecat lay curled up on the bed, asleep.

I'm sure you realize we are of Jewish descent.

Yes, I know.

There's still time for you to turn back.

She had sold many a bit of merchandise in her life. She knew when it was too late for a customer to walk away from the deal. The more freedom you gave him to choose, the more likely he was to choose exactly what he was supposed to.

What are you saying?

For a while both of them remained standing beside the bed of the absent girl, looking at the cat, which, from time to time, extended its claws in a dream and then pulled them back in again beneath the fur.

That morning, for the sake of her daughter's happiness, she had sold her daughter's happiness. Sometimes the price one pays for something continues to grow after the fact, becoming too expensive long after it has been paid. A transaction like this is a living equilibrium, she's grasped this in the course of the three years since her son-in-law's disappearance. Profit and loss must avail themselves of a salesman if they are to work together, but fundamentally their dealings are with one another; at some point they balance each other out again. In the sunlit silence of a Sabbath, a letter falls from an opening hand into a hand that someone is holding out. A man wanting to deliver a letter on Shabbat is not permitted to, according to the Talmud, because that would be work. It would be work to walk from the street into a building, in other words mixing indoors and outdoors. On Shabbat people are to rest, and the three spaces—Outside, Inside, Wilderness—are to be kept separate from each other. But if the messenger walks up to the recipient's window opening onto the street and lets the letter fall into the recipient's hand, the messenger would not be leaving his space—the street—and the recipient would be remaining in his own—the building; what's more, the dropping of the letter would not be a giving, nor would its receipt in the open hand be a taking. How heatedly she and her husband had debated with her parents about how the Talmud pointed the way here to deceit, to the violation of the rules that were supposed to be its jurisdiction. Her father said it was a matter of how the boundaries were defined, that it wasn't possible to comply with a prohibition unless you knew exactly where it started and ended. In any case, it wasn't a parable, her husband had said, but rather in the end pure mathematics. Her mother had laughed and opined: thank goodness it was a letter the messenger was dropping and not an egg. She herself had declared the messenger's hesitation pedantic, making her father smile at her indignation, saying: you don't understand what's meant. At the time she didn't want to understand what was meant, her father was still alive, and as long as that was the case she—even as a grown woman—was the one permitted to be in error. In the sunlit silence of a Sabbath, a letter falls from an opening hand into a hand that someone is holding out.

How happy a person must be, she's come to think—now that twenty years have passed since her husband's fatal beating, three since her daughter's abandonment, one and a half since her father's death and burial—how happy a person must be who can manage to comport himself as impassively as the messenger in this story, simply letting things happen as they will and nonetheless delivering what has been entrusted to him. When in her home she finds traces of dirt on a knife that her elderly mother has cleaned, she feels only disgust. Her daughter, on the other hand, moves so lethargically about the shop that she often feels an impulse to drag her by the hair back to work. But she observes even her own body with impatience as it struggles to hoist the ten-kilogram sacks of flour onto the cart, and the farmers who sometimes help her and sometimes don't are called Marek, Krzystof, or often—hearing the name is still difficult for her—Andrei.

18

So what began with the hands is now ending with the hands. Should she perhaps give a present to the man who thought she was for sale? Certainly not, she thinks, and, after he's gone, she takes the money from the chest of drawers, leaves the room, goes downstairs, out of the building (which looks no different from others), and onto the street. She gives the money to the first beggar woman she sees squatting beside the road, and for two days afterward life really does look just the same as before. But on the third day, a Sunday, the officer comes into the shop again as if nothing ever happened, he wants to buy matches, he says, the same as always, in the back room her mother is wrapping merchandise in newsprint, it rustles, then he reaches across the counter to grab his recent lover by the chin, forcing her to look him in the eye and says, not even lowering his voice, he has a friend who would also be interested.

Rustling newspaper.

The day, the time, the building that looks like any other.

Rustling newspaper.

If she doesn't want anyone to hear of this, he says, she should keep the appointment.

Silence.

Child, can you give me a hand here?

Yes, Mother.

Admit it, you enjoyed it too.

What a disaster—child, where are you? My hand's about to fall off.

Coming!

19

After the inspection of the immigrating flesh, the mind, too, is checked; man, woman, and child must answer thirty questions, and only persons giving acceptable answers will be allowed to cross over to the mainland. Madness, melancholia, anarchism—all these and others like them will be rejected. Were you ever in prison? Do you practice polygamy? In his now rumpled coat, the Austrian asks himself whether in America, as a result of this strict examination at the border, there are no longer deficiencies of any sort, no longer any cripples or incurable diseases, no madness, no insubordination, perhaps even no death?

20

So that's how it was when you fell off the edge of the *palatschinke*, a grain of sugar, and disappeared. Already after her second customer she started using the money to buy something for herself, a pair of stockings, after all it was her own body she was offering up for sale. After the third, a scarf—leave the curtains open, I want to look at you—after the fourth—listen, can't you struggle a little—and the fifth—bring your mouth here—and the sixth—you Jewish sow: four, five, and six together, a new pair of shoes. It hurt, it disgusted her, it was ludicrous, sometimes her skin felt like it was cracking open in delicate spots and burning, but bit by bit taking leave of her senses became her job. Now she knew what the men were hiding from their families, and the ones she ran into on the street wearing their uniforms, or in top hats, or work smocks—never again was she able to see them as anything other than what they all finally were: naked. What she could buy with the money she earned in this way—considering that she would never again be at one with any person in the world, not even with herself—was absurdly little. But the less a dress, a hat, or piece of jewelry stood in any sort of relationship to what she was giving of herself, the easier it became for her to sell herself the next time. Eventually her true worth, which now only she would know, would be impossible to measure. *How delightful the gods find these penitent sinners; / lifting prodigal children in arms made of fire / with jubilant cries up to Heaven above.* Her mother never asked where all the new things she wore came from, but even without being asked, she told her she had found the shoes for a good price here or there, already used, or that a girlfriend had given her one or the other trinket, that she found the ring in the street. Hadn't her mother also lied to her about the death of her father throughout her childhood and youth?

21

Waiting for the results of the examination, a thousand or two thousand people sit in the gloomy light of the great hall, and new ones are constantly coming to join them. These people squat, lie on the ground, or sit on benches: people with bundles, bedding, and crates, with samovars, people without any baggage at all, children running about, crying babies, people who have lain down on the floor and gone to sleep, people with frail parents, people who understand not a word of English, people who don't know whether the person who's supposed to pick them up here is really coming, people who are filled with hope, with despair, people who are homesick, frightened, people who don't know what's in store for them, people who are wondering where they'll find the twenty-five dollars for their immigration fee, people who suddenly want to go back, or who are just glad that the ground beneath their feet is no longer swaying, people with long or short pants, with head-scarves, skirts, suits, hats, with fringe, shoes, or slippers, gloves or cuffs, with braids, beards, mustaches, curls, parted hair, people with many, few, or no children—countless people, all of whom are waiting for the moment when eventually their names will be called and they will learn whether they are allowed to stay or will be sent back to Europe. The young man, who is also one of those waiting, thinks: This is probably more or less the way it's going to be one day at the Last Judgment.

And then, suddenly, a loud clattering and jangling fills the hall; everyone falls silent for a moment, looks over, and sees a large Chinese vase lying shattered on the ground—a girl has dropped it in one of the very few places in the hall not covered with people or clothes or bundles, but only with stone tiles, she has dropped this vase that she carried in her arms ever since her departure from a small town outside Bucharest or Warsaw, or outside Vienna or Odessa or Athens or Paris—all the long way via Bremen, Antwerp, Danzig, Marseille, Piraeus, or Barcelona: The vase has shattered into bits here in the arrival hall, the final stop before New York, for the girl has just—for the first time in her life—seen a man with dark skin, who happened to be walking across the room with a broom in his hand, and she must have thought it was the Devil. The girl's mother now looks as if she would like best to strike her child dead, and the girl looks as though she wishes she were dead. Then the noise recommences—the crying, talking, and shouting—the children go back to running around, the adults wait, and a boy, having been given an ice cream by a relative who got permission to visit him, places the ice cream on the bench, and there it melts, because the boy doesn't know what ice cream is.

Hey look, the inspector wrote a letter on your back in chalk—mine too?

The boy turns his back to his friend so he can see whether he too has a mark on him, one that may possibly decide if he will be permitted to stay or be sent back to Europe.

No, there's nothing on your back.

What sort of letter is it, do you think?

Dunno.

So do I have to go back now, or do you?

No idea.

Two little girls are crouching on the floor.

I'm thirsty.

Grandmother says that when you get to Battery Park, there are a lot of fountains there.

Good, I'll have a drink then.

No, you mustn't drink, whatever happens.

How come?

She says that then you'll forget everything you ever knew about where you come from.

Then I'll forget the garden?

Yes.

And the fireplace?

Yes.

And Grandfather?

Yes.

And Grandmother?

Yes.

And the cat?

Yes.

Everything?

Yes.

How does Grandmother know?

Someone told her.

22

One evening, after one day, there is no dinner on the table; when mother and daughter try to open the door to Grandmother's room, it isn't possible, because her body is lying in front of it. *Vos iz mit dir? Mamele, vos iz mit dir? Mamele,* what's the matter? Simon the coachman is called, and he breaks open the door with an axe, with Mother standing beside him, one hand pressed to her mouth; her daughter calls her grandmother's name, but no one answers.

What else have you got to do today?

I have a guest to look after.

Do you have a lot of guests?

Is the lonely soul not a guest in the body? Today it's here, and by tomorrow it's on its way again.

When the hole in the door is finally big enough, the two women stick their hands through, reaching for Grandmother, but she is already cold, as cold as only something dead feels.

23

At the many small, rectangular teller windows in the great hall at Ellis Island, a Loshel becomes a Louis, a Davnar a David, an Arden an Alvin, a Chaia a Clara. And he, Johann, becomes a Joe. Did he really want to go that far? And why is he doing this? Others learn at similar rectangular windows that their families will be permitted to stay here but they themselves must go back, or that because of them, the whole family will be sent back along with them, returning home to a place where they no longer want to make their home, where they'll starve or be beaten to death. Then they start shouting or cling to one another, while others just stand there quietly, weeping or falling silent altogether.

24

Only after her grandmother's funeral does her mother tell her that she, the daughter, took her very first steps holding her grandmother's hand.

And where were you?

I was making all the preparations for us to move while also keeping the shop open.

No one was helping you?

No.

Why not?

We were moving in the wrong direction.

So a mother knows more about a child than a child could ever know about herself. If her own child were still alive, she, as the child's mother, would surely have been the one to teach her how to put one foot in front of the other—and on some morning or other when her husband was at the office, the child, holding her hand, would have managed the journey from wardrobe to chest without falling for the first time ever, or if the weather were fair, perhaps the route would have led from the front door to the corner. As a mother, she would know this and never forget, and then one day she would perhaps tell her child, or perhaps not, with or without a reason. But now her secrets and memories are hers alone, and no one's going to ask her, even many years later, about the things she keeps to herself. Her grandmother's house, where, she's just been told, she learned to walk, has now collapsed—she saw it herself not long ago. The roof crashed down into the parlor, turning what was formerly a room into a garbage heap. Chickens now mince about on the heap, poking the rotting thatch with their beaks on their chicken-life-long search for worms and bugs. If she were to remain in this town of modest size her whole life, she would, sooner or later, come out of a building that looks like any other and find herself right in front of her mother, or perhaps a neighbor or friend, even that would be enough. No, unable to find herself, she has no need to wait for others to give her up for lost. She's already free down to her bones; already it's a matter of complete indifference what she does.

With the same hands she used when she was learning to walk to hold tight to her grandmother so as not to lose her balance, she now packs a few necessities in a suitcase, carries it to the station, and pays for the ticket. In a second-class compartment she travels over rails whose maintenance used to be the responsibility of one who was called her husband in her earlier life, putting this leg of the journey behind her takes only an hour and twenty minutes; then she travels for an additional two hours, not getting out until Lemberg—capital of the Kingdom of Galicia and Lodomeria—ninety kilometers southeast of the small border town where she was first a girl, then a young woman, and then, for a brief period, even a mother and wife. She copies out an address from a notice hanging at the station, carries her suitcase there, pays half the first month's rent in advance, presses down a door handle, and in this way enters her new lodgings. Here no one knows who held her hand when she learned to walk upright at only eleven months, nor does anyone know that the Poles are to blame for her inability to remember a father, nor even that she can still recite all of Goethe's poem "The God and the Bayadère" by heart. Here she will use her right hand, and of course also her left, as well as her mouth and the other orifices of her body for no other purpose than to keep this body alive, along with the hands, the mouth, and the rest to which these orifices are attached. To be sure, she will do this under a new name—one that, in her opinion, seems reasonably appropriate to her new life, and if anyone asks her name, she says it's *Missy von Lemberg* and laughs.

25

Admittedly, the Austro-Hungarian monarchy assembled almost as many different ethnic groups under its crown as he was seeing here in the great hall. From Bosnia to the most remote Polish-speaking provinces, the doors of a tobacco shop were invariably adorned with black and yellow stripes, with the Kaiser's portrait occupying a place of honor on the wall. Yet, for all the intermingling of different languages and dialects, German remained the language of bureaucracy. The Kaiser, though, hadn't selected the individuals to be let in; rather, he'd swallowed up entire peoples indiscriminately, making all of them part of his realm. Melancholia, madness, and unlawfulness remained at home—even after home became suddenly known as Austria or Hungary—and it did the monarchy no harm. Europe's peoples, with or without wars, had always crisscrossed the continent, intermixing and seeking out new homes whenever their one bit of land produced too little or life became unbearable for some reason. But perhaps a coastline like this was a more naturally defined border. Here you could send the people you didn't want back out on the water, even if it meant they would perish back home or simply drown at sea like surplus kittens.

26

For the first time ever she wishes she were of limited intelligence—limited enough that she might bring herself to call her daughter an ingrate. Her apartment now has so many spare rooms that it's worth her while to rent them out. She gives up the shop, takes her leave of the farmers, and sells horse and cart to Simon, the coachman. She removes all personal items from the rooms and even clears out the cellar a little at a time, reasoning that in two or three years she may no longer have the strength for work like this. She now finally gives away many things that she intended to save although she had no plans for their use, such as the cradle in which her grandchild slept for eight months, the ivory toy with the little silver bells, even the woolen shawl she gave her daughter to wrap around her shoulders, which had never once been used, since her daughter hadn't had the chance to go out for walks with her baby in the park. She keeps the footstool, for without it she can no longer reach the top shelf of her bookcase where volumes 1 to 20 of Goethe's *Collected Works* still are and will remain, including Volume 9, which was struck by Andrei's stone years before. (And so the bad memory remains preserved among the good, one as incorporeal as the others.) She also keeps her mother's silver candelabra, it stands now on the window-sill in the parlor, but she never lights the candles on a Sabbath or on any other day.

27

It's August, and he sets foot on solid ground again on the other side of the world. Heat is collecting between the buildings; his wife would have called this air thick enough to cut, he would have stolen a glance at the ink-colored shadows beneath her arms on her other-wise light-blue dress and when no one was looking, slipped his hand in, and she would have said, cut it out, and laughed. Now he is see-ing here for the first time peddlers with nothing but soiled under-shirts covering their sweaty torsos, calling out their fruit, meat, or fish, holding up a sample in the air, the customers in these parts seem not to be put off by the casually rampant hair on chests, the backs of necks, and arms, exposed unbidden to their view. He himself goes into a hotel in search of a clean lavatory, on the ferry from El-lis Island to Battery Park, his hair was blown into disarray; he looks at himself in the mirror, seeing the same man who was in the mir-ror back in Europe, and he arranges the strands of this man's hair, dabs a bit of pomade on his mustache, drapes the coat made of good Imperial and Royal cloth over his arm, puts the suitcase in his other hand, and sends the man out again into the open air, already almost perfectly American. The slip of paper his traveling companion gave him when they parted has directions and an address written on it. Here and there he catches a glimpse of the enormous figure as he walks, but viewed from between the buildings, she looks almost like a castaway signaling for help with her torch, possibly out of fear of sinking, for the island on which she's been stranded is hardly bigger than a handkerchief compared to the size of her feet. He turns right, as instructed on the paper, and immediately finds the recommended entrance to an underground tunnel; he's to travel on something called a *subway* to Harlem, which is where his traveling companion has his factory; the deeper he descends, the hotter and staler the subterranean air, back in the monarchy they used to sing a tune by Mozart: *Forever true and honest be / unto the chilly grave, / and stray not by a finger's breadth / from God's anointed way*—here, by contrast, even the dead must be sweating in the depths of their graves. He tries to remember the rest of the verses to the song, but then the car, drawn by horses, arrives in the station, the unfortunate beasts are wearing blinders even though it's already quite dark underground, Simon the coachman would shake his head. He himself, the traveler, is scarcely less deaf and dumb than the horses, he neither speaks nor understands a single English word, he doesn't know whose image is on the coin he uses to pay his fare, and he takes the gum-chewing of his fellow passengers for an illness. And now, having come to understand that the world of numerals conceals more than it displays, he reads: 96th, 110th, 116th Street. Only once before had he known this little where he stood: during his childhood when his father would beat him Sunday after Sunday, without his ever being told the reason, not even later, when he was made to thank his father for the beating, addressing him as "Sir" and with his title, Superior Customs Officer. His mother had failed to protect her son from her own husband, she had watched his beating, but only stood there in the corner without stirring from the spot, quietly weeping. Whenever her weeping became too loud, she got a beating as well. As a child, he didn't know whom to hate more: his father, who did his best to beat him to death every Sunday, or his mother, who just stood there and didn't know what to do. His wife, too, hadn't known what to do on the night in question.

Back home, his mother died even before he finished his degree at the Technical University in Vienna—died of a stroke, he read in the telegram he received there. Even today the word makes him want to ask: a stroke with what weapon—a bad joke, but he knew the power of his father's fists. Bruises like the ones his father surely gave his mother continue to change color in the coffin, he'd heard once from a friend who was studying medicine, in the ground they turn first green and then finally yellow, as though this metamorphosis of colors were standing in, if only briefly, for the sorts of development of which the person who'd been struck dead by violent hands was no longer capable. At the time, he'd been about to sit for his exams for his intermediate degree in weights and measures, and for this reason he did not attend the funeral, to which his father raised no objection. Somewhere he'd once learned or read that New York was built on stone, perhaps this is why he wants to stay here, for on rocky ground he can be quite sure of not following in anyone's footsteps: neither those of his father, the Superior Customs Officer, nor those of his timorous mother.

28

Now it's like this: The one hand knows that a man's member doesn't hurt when you squeeze it, even applying a fair bit of pressure, it's just a muscle. Another hand has known for a long time that caution is required when pouring water over the kasha in the pot, because the water can splash up and possibly scald you. One hand grasps the handle of a drill in a factory eight hundred times a day. One hand washes the other, another gets slipped through a person's hair, another drops a quarter into a gas meter. One hand pulls a sheet taut, another wipes crumbs from the table, a third flips a light switch. One pair of eyes sees dust motes rising in a beam of light, another peers into men's wide-open mouths, another notices a little can of oil. Ears hear a door being slammed, sirens, someone coughing; feet slide into silk stockings, elbows are massaged, toenails are cut, filed, and polished, feet are so blistered they won't fit in the shoes; gray, black, brown hair; rings under eyes; calluses; two weary breasts; almost a proper bald spot; toothache; tongue; a voice like silk. What under other circumstances might have been or become a family has now been torn so far asunder that being drawn and quartered by horses would be nothing in comparison. Nonetheless, one or the other of them—here, there or yonder—sometimes thinks the very same thought: Why was the baby so quiet all of a sudden?

INTERMEZZO

But if, for example, the child's mother or father had thrust open the window in the middle of the night, had scooped a handful of snow from the sill, and put it under the baby's shirt, perhaps the child would suddenly have started breathing again, possibly cried again as well, in any case its heart might have gone back to beating, its skin would have grown warm and the snow melted on its chest. Possibly something like divine inspiration was required, although where such inspiration might come from was something neither mother nor father knew. One glance out the night-dark window at the shimmering snow, or even just the creaking of the window frame contracting in the cold, a sound made by the cold window at precisely the moment the child fell silent, might have sufficed for inspiration, instead of the same sound occurring just half an hour afterward when it was too late. In secondary school, the child's mother had learned that the Pythia had answered the question posed by Croesus, king of Lydia, with *If you cross the Halys, you will destroy a great empire*. But what the Pythia did with all the answers no one requested is something the infant's mother wouldn't have been able to say, nor the father either. Probably the eternal oracle sat eternally above the *pneuma* rising from the earth's interior and watched as her own silence grew in size, attaining inhuman proportions. If an inspiration had come to these parents, the child's survival would have become just that. The weave of life in its entirety—containing all knowledge of snow, all glances out the window, all listening to sounds made by the cold or damp wood—would have severed one truth from the other for all time. Only the blue tinge of the girl's skin—above all around her mouth and chin—would have stayed with the parents, an uncomfortable memory. A memory that would have returned to them uninvited now and then, and neither would have mentioned it to the other, for fear of tempting fate. And so fate would have kept quiet, and this first moment when the child might have died would have passed without further ado.

The little girl would have learned to walk holding her mother's hand, her first steps taking her from the wardrobe to the chest; her great-grandmother would have braided her hair, singing a little song about a man who makes a coat out of an old piece of cloth, then when it's gotten tattered he makes a vest out of the coat, then makes a scarf from the tattered vest, a cap from the tattered scarf, a button from the tattered cap, a nothing at all from the button, and in the end he makes this song out of the nothing at all, but by then the braids would have been finished; and the girl's grandmother would have brought her store-bought sweets or homemade challah. Four years later, her little sister would have been born, but her father would still have remained in the eleventh pay-grade, by now he would have known every last one of the larger trees along his section of rail that had ever dropped a branch on the tracks, and her mother, since they were unable to afford a maid or laundress, would have run the household all on her own, washing their laundry herself in a big pot in her kitchen so that no one would see. In the evenings, she would have fallen asleep over a book she was trying to read, still holding it in her hand. The girl's grandmother, seeing her daughter struggle, would sometimes have slipped her a little money, and on the occasion of her daughter's seventh wedding anniversary in 1908, she'd have given the young family a trip to Vienna for the Corpus Christi procession, where, with a little luck, one might catch a glimpse of the old Kaiser walking as an ordinary sinner behind his canopy Heaven. Her daughter would have hesitated to accept the gift, but in the end, the father would have applied for a certificate of domicile for himself, his wife, and his two girls. Proudly they would have traveled together for the first time over the rails for which the father was responsible, passing all the large trees that had dropped branches during storms over the last several years, this leg of the journey took an hour and twenty minutes, but the trip as a whole was seventeen hours.

In Vienna then, in the middle of the crowd lining the streets all the way from St. Stephen's to the Hofburg, the child's father would have run into a former classmate, who was meanwhile employed at the Viennese Imperial and Royal Central Institution for Meteorology; the men would have embraced and launched into tales of how their lives had unfolded since they last parted; her father would have said all sorts of things, but not this one: Just imagine, my wife took a handful of snow and saved our daughter's life. He would have kept silent on this score, not wanting to challenge fate. The two men would have reminisced about what a wonderful time they'd had studying in Vienna, how they'd been "bed lodgers" for a while, actually sharing the bed of a shift worker who was never there at night: one of them would sleep in the bed for four hours, from ten at night until two in the morning, then the other one would sleep from two until six, and when one of them fell asleep during the morning lecture, the other would prop a few books under his head to keep him comfortable. They would have also remembered how on winter weekends they often went for walks along the snowy trails of the Vienna Woods and on one occasion they noticed the difference in the prints they were leaving behind. Deep in conversation, they stopped walking and happened to turn around, and there was the serpentine track left by his companion, while his own prints formed a perfectly straight line. At the time they'd been surprised and asked themselves what this could mean. Even today they don't know the answer. Each of them would have assured the other how extraordinary it was that they still felt so close, even though more than eight years had passed since they'd last seen each other and they hadn't even kept in touch by letter, indeed they'd practically forgotten one another, if truth be told. A friendship sealed up like a jar of preserves, her father would have said, and his former classmate would have laughed and, when he was done laughing, he would have remarked how long it had been since he had laughed like that. Then they would have spoken of their jobs, of the envious colleagues, the resentments, the vagaries of the Confidential Qualification, and his friend would have said how different things used to be—as a student, he would never have believed how closely one had to watch what one said, making it almost impossible to find true friends later in life. Her father would have nodded, saying that he, too, had been lonely these past eight years, excepting of course his relationship with his wife—and here he would have tightened his grip on his wife's arm, without mentioning, to be sure, her religious affiliation. His university friend would now have looked at the woman more closely and then remarked that the joys of family life had unfortunately not yet been granted him, but, well, at least he was lucky at cards, by which he meant to say: in his career, of course, well, you can't have it all, then he said "well" again, not following it with any further observation. The father would have been unsure what to say next, but his former classmate would have gone on to inform him that at the moment the Institution for Meteorology was looking for someone who could perform various writing tasks, and probably it wasn't any better a job than the one he already had, as it was also an eleventh pay-grade position, but there were bonuses, and at least it was in Vienna—Vienna!—and he could certainly try to be of service to his friend, assuming of course that he really did want to live in Vienna—Vienna!—though to be sure the city did not come cheap, especially for a family, there would have to be some tightening of belts, alas: Vienna! So think it over ... my goodness, I'd be truly ... don't mention it ... if you could, I don't know how I, etc. The younger daughter would have been showing signs of impatience all this time, finally tugging more firmly on her father's hand, asking him to lift her up on his shoulders. He would have lifted her up and then several times warmly thanked his rediscovered friend, who wouldn't have wanted to accept the thanks, after all he had no idea whether he could really, but he'd make an effort, and possibly.... Right after this, the Kaiser would have appeared, walking behind his heavenly canopy, an ordinary sinner, and the family from the provinces would have cheered like all the rest, and already no one would have been able to distinguish them from actual Viennese. As soon as they arrived back at the rooming house where they were staying, her father would have written an official letter of application and mailed it off that very evening.

His colleagues in Brody—above all his immediate superior, Chief Inspector First Class of the Eighth Rank Vinzenz Knorr—would have been quite astonished to hear of his transfer several weeks later. The grandmother would have accompanied the family to the station for their second and now final departure for Vienna, and waving goodbye, she would have been fully conscious of the fact that, along with her daughter, all her questions about her missing father were now traveling away, and that this was no doubt for the best.

BOOK II

1

In January 1919, the gold buttons on the father's coat still display the double-headed eagle and the Kaiser's crown, but the Kaiser has been dead two years now, and the eagle's Hungarian half has long since flown away. But the coat still keeps him warm, so he remains wrapped in Imperial and Royal finery, sitting day after day in his underheated, now-democratic office in the Meteorological Institution in Vienna; and after work he goes from there to the underheated coffeehouse *Vindobona* for two games of chess with his friend and colleague, sitting in his coat there as well. Even at home in the evenings he doesn't take off this coat, for the wood that mother and daughter gather in the Vienna Woods twice a week is damp, and when it's stuffed into the kitchen stove it hisses more than it burns. The heating stoves in the parlor, the bedroom and the room shared by the two girls have remained cold for a long time. The father sits down at the table in his coat with the gold buttons, there are boiled potatoes for dinner, one each, for father, mother, and the younger daughter.

Where's the big one?

She's not home.

Do you remember when you were her age? That's when things started between us.

That's enough now.

2

You look like a whore, the mother had said to her older daughter the previous summer when she shortened her skirt to above the knee and wanted to leave the house like that.

What do you know about whores? her daughter had shouted and slammed the door so hard on her way out, the panes of glass in the upper half rattled. After her daughter left, the mother sat there weeping for half an hour, but then she hiked her own skirt up to above her knees and looked at her legs in the mirror. After four years of war, Vienna had gone to seed, and so had she. She'd been so filled with hope when she had traveled here all alone. Once her husband's transfer was certain, she'd come to look for an apartment. She still remembers the first time she walked into this building smelling of limestone and dust, a limestone and dust smell that only the buildings of a metropolis can have. It was shadowy and cool in the building's entryway, while outside, the heat was so thick you could cut it with a knife. If her husband had come with her, he would have quickly slipped his hand into her armpit when no one was looking, and she would have said, cut it out, and laughed. Before she climbed the two flights of stairs to inspect the apartment, she had run her hand over the head of the eagle at the bottom of the banister, perhaps it would bring her luck. Two bedrooms with a view of the public baths across the way, the kitchen and one bedroom facing the courtyard—the girls could play down there—a shared water tap and a separate toilet in the stairwell. The apartment was affordable, one month's rent in advance. Then she went home again to pack for the move. The last thing she packed was the footstool her grandmother had given her for her household; the first thing she would do when she arrived would be to place this footstool in the vestibule of the new apartment, and from then on Vienna would be her home. When her mother wrote her two or three years later that for the maneuvers taking place on the border they were now using live ammunition, perhaps a war was coming, she hadn't worried. They had fled from the provinces to Vienna as if taking refuge on an enormous ship, but it would never have occurred to them to suspect that this ship was already beginning to sink. *Fire, locusts, leeches, plague, bears, foxes, snakes, insects, lice* were names that had often been given to Jews here in Vienna, but she hadn't known that. *God our Father whom we love, you gave us teeth, now give us food.* Perhaps the eagle at the bottom of the banister was really a vulture that had been waiting all these years for her demise; in any case she's been fighting back for years now, refusing to let her family be turned into fodder, but this requires all her strength—strength she has, and also strength she hasn't had for a long time now. She's stopped plucking the hairs on her legs, her toenails are hard, her calves full of blue veins. In the parks of Vienna, the grass grows knee-high in summer, open squares are used to grow carrots, potatoes, and turnips, the countryside is sweeping its way across Vienna, wiping away the city, and no one much cares as long as he himself survives, there isn't enough life left to spend correcting and clipping away at life. *And try your arm, as a boy beheads thistles, against oak-trees and mountain heights.* In summer, Arenberg Park is barely distinguishable from the meadows surrounding Brody near the Russian border, but now she's grown up and has other things to do than breaking off a hazel switch and scything the grass with it as she crosses a field (as she used to so as not to overlook the edge of the *palatschinke*). They didn't escape to Vienna to starve there. But no one can predict when it will be revealed that a wish is going to be left unfulfilled.

I've got just a few more things to copy out, he tells his wife.

That's all right, she says, and leaves the kitchen.

As the following chronicle documents, the Styrian ground shook for thirty days. The most extensive of these shocks were recorded on days when disturbances that originated in the area around Laibach were felt in our region as well.

67

The little one—she's still called this by her parents even though she's over thirteen now and nearly five foot seven—is out in the vestibule preparing for her nighttime shift standing in line; she clamps a blanket under her arm, and her mother straps the folding chair to her back. A *lange loksh*. After she leaves, her mother goes to sleep for a few hours before midnight when it's her turn to take her daughter's place in line. With any luck, after standing in line all night long, they'll be given cow udder at seven in the morning. Udder is edible if you boil it in milk.

The big one's bed is empty.

3

Most definitely she was not a whore. Already the year before last she'd have been able to sell herself for two pairs of shoes, and recently also for one liter of cream, fifteen potatoes, or a half pound of fat. Again and again she'd had her price whispered in her ear by one or the other black marketeer, a price that—like all prices—was constantly in flux according to the prevailing rates of exchange, a flux that invariably maintained a downward trend. She could have sold herself long ago to keep her family from freezing at home, or for her sister, who was growing faster than she should. Perhaps in the end her mother was angry with her for doing exactly the opposite of what she reproached her daughter for: still trying to be young without selling herself. On the banks of the Danube one night the previous summer, she'd let someone unbutton her blouse for the first time, a younger schoolmate had slipped his hand under the fabric and touched her breasts, but that's all she'd permitted, after all, he was practically a child. Another night the previous summer, her father's friend had met her once in secret and said he found her red hair more alluring than anything he'd seen in all his

68

life, and then he'd kissed her hair and finally her shoulder, but that's all she'd permitted, after all, he was too old. Possibly the man destined for her was just falling in battle on the banks of the Marne or the Soča, bleeding to death in the barbed wire outside Verdun, or losing his legs. This war was shooting her youth to pieces as she was still marching through it. Her best friend had gotten engaged to a university student who had been called up; for two years he had fought battle after battle and now he lay in a field hospital with gas poisoning. Someone should declare war on war, but how that was supposed to work, she didn't know, and neither did her friend. In the food lines she'd seen mothers hold up their starving children in front of the soldiers on duty, threatening to hang them from the window frame and themselves as well, or to take care of the entire family at once by drowning everyone in the Danube; one of them had even laid her infant down in the street, refusing to pick the baby up again because she didn't know how she could go on feeding it. Once, when the daughter was to return home empty-handed after hours of waiting, she felt such fury that she called on the other women to march on the *Rathaus* with her to complain, she'd waved her handkerchief in the air above her head like a flag, and sure enough, hundreds of desperate women fell into step behind her—a girl of only fourteen. But for several hours, no one came out of the *Rathaus* to negotiate with them, and the women—who still had to find something to feed their families that day—gradually scattered and dispersed. She, on the other hand, had sat down right where she was and wept, using the handkerchief that had served as her flag to blow her nose and dry her tears. She hadn't told her mother of this defeat, but instead had resolved that very day to make herself independent of hunger, to stop letting her own body blackmail her into failure, and the less she ate—this is something she'd already noticed—the clearer her thoughts became. In the end her perceptions were so heightened that during the nights of that last summer, lying with her best friend on the banks of the

Danube pretending to be young, she heard not only the river's current but even the fish and snakes gliding beneath the water's surface, clairvoyant with hunger she knew how the creatures in the river's depths coiled around each other, snapping and hissing.

4

He wasn't the only human being in the world who had an inkling of how everything was connected to everything else, otherwise, he'd have chosen dying over freezing and watching his family freeze, starving and watching his family starve. *A remarkable phenomenon of the cycle of tremors beginning with the 1895 Easter earthquake in Laibach is that some of the aftershocks continued for quite some time afterward, taking a significant toll in certain areas, and displaying phenomena similar to those of the main tremor. The earthquake of April 5, 1897, though not particularly strong, was distinguished by the motion of the ground being less pronounced than the shock's acoustic effects.* In any case, he would have to remain alive until at least the first of the next month, because then his wife would receive his salary. One month's salary, if she stretched it skillfully, would last a week. What would happen during the remaining three weeks of that month and the weeks of the following one, and what in the world would happen after that—this he did not know. *The tremor consisted of two shocks from below, the first of which was stronger; each lasted for approximately 2 sec. with a 1 sec. interval between; according to observations, the shaking appeared to be directed from north to south and was accompanied by a sound like that of a cart being driven into a building's entryway; this preceded the tremor by several seconds and was longer in duration. Clocks and lamps vibrated.*

He cuts the tips off his gloves so he can hold the pen better. When the ink begins to solidify in the cold, he breathes on the nib.

5

In November, the war was declared over, and in December her friend's fiancé finally returned home. One afternoon he was suddenly standing there at the door, and at first the girls didn't even realize that they knew him, that's how much he'd changed. Even weeks after his return they saw how it pained him when someone scattered crumbs for the pigeons in the park. When they asked him about the war, he refused to answer, he'd just take one of the cigarette stubs he'd collected somewhere out of his jacket pocket and start smoking. When they told him they wanted to go out, he didn't mind, he just stayed home. And when in January the curfew was changed from ten p.m. to eight, they would often simply remain in her friend's apartment to save the twenty heller coin they'd have to slip the concierge to be let in after curfew. They would drink and talk, sometimes she even stayed the night, sleeping on a mattress in the vestibule. On those few evenings when she went out without her friend, she refused to let anyone touch, much less kiss her.

6

At night, the younger daughter sits in the street, waiting for midnight to come. Indeed, she's been sitting like this for years, sometimes with her mother, sometimes with her sister, and often alone. This waiting began soon after the start of the war—first for bread, meat, and fat, and later also for sugar, milk, potatoes, eggs, and coal. The war is over, and still she's sitting here, just the same as before, in this dark forest of bodies that has been growing up all around her for the past five years, stretching its limbs further with each passing night into alleyways and streets, around corners, up steps, and across the squares of Vienna, while she herself has grown within it, grown to five foot seven now, shooting up like a bean-pole despite the starvation, and for years spending night after night waiting amid thousands of others who, by waiting, were fighting for survival: in front of market halls, Ankerbrot bakeries, butcher shops, and flour distribution centers, waiting in front of the various points of sale maintained by the milk industry, and also in front of shops offering carbide, candles, shoes, coffee, or soap; they stood, lay, and sat everywhere: either in silence or murmuring, the blood of Vienna beginning to stir as morning approached, to push and shove, to kick and curse, to elbow its way forward, to complain, persevere, bite, or scratch until the obstacle fell away flailing, then was pushed aside, pushing others, screeching, crying, mocking, and falling into despair. Five foot seven, while others had become weak or old during these same nights, while some had gone insane or fallen into a stupor—a few had even died while they were wait-ing. She sits here on her folding chair, enjoying the fact that the cobblestones are so uneven that she can rock back and forth on the chair, she sits wrapped in a blanket, waiting for midnight when her mother will relieve her.

7

Sometimes when his wife retires so early in the evening, he goes over after she's fallen asleep and watches her. *In three homes, ordinary Swiss clocks whose pendulums swung in a north-south orientation stopped.* When she sleeps, she does not speak. That's all right, she says to him when she is awake, when he—after remarking that the sky is either overcast, blue, cloudy, or perfectly clear—announces that now he'll be coming home earlier, because the office will no longer be heated after two in the afternoon. But when she's asleep he likes to sit down beside her bed and make one further attempt to get to the bottom of what has seemed to him the greatest riddle in all the history of mankind: how processes, circumstances, or events of a general nature—such as war, famine, or even a civil servant's salary that fails to increase along with the galloping inflation—can infiltrate a private face. Here they turn a few hairs gray, there devour a pair of lovely cheeks until the skin is stretched taut across angular jawbones; the secession of Hungary, say, might result in a pair of lips bitten raw in the case of one particular woman, perhaps even his own wife. In other words, there is a constant translation between far outside and deep within, it's just that a different vocabulary exists for each of us, which no doubt explains why it's never been noticed that this is a language in the first place—and in fact, the only language valid across the world and for all time. If a person were to study a sufficient number of faces, he would surely be able to observe wrinkles, twitching eyelids, lusterless teeth, and draw conclusions about the death of a Kaiser, unjust reparations payments, or a stabilizing social democracy. His wife doesn't ask why he brought *Notes on Earthquakes in Styria* home with him, why he spends evening after evening reading this book and copying out the most important passages; the thing is, it describes in meticulous detail exactly the sorts of processes he is now able to see with completely different eyes: How one and the same cause can have a thousand different effects on different regions and locations. It feels to him as if the top layer is crumbling away all at once from everything he sees and encounters, a layer that once prevented him from comprehending, and finally he is able to recognize what lies below. *Minds = landscape*, he notes between one passage and the next. What a happy coincidence that these observations happened to fall into his hands: the hands of one who has taken it upon himself to investigate this primeval tongue—that's what he's calling it—for as long as his strength holds up. *Persons standing upon solid ground detected*

73

a faint vibration of the earth. Nothing else is keeping him here in this miserable life in which a civil servant, ninth class, is forced to stand by and watch his family starve.

8

Good, now wash your hands and you'll be ready.

Is there water left?

Yes.

Well, all right then.

The water half-filling the bucket is covered in a thin layer of ice.

What a disaster.

Not to worry.

The old woman pokes her hands through the layer of ice into the water and washes them.

Goodness gracious, that's cold.

And then: Hat, scarf, glove.

Oh, your boots.

I almost forgot my feet....

And with all the snow.

What a disaster. Don't worry, I'll manage, I'll be fine.

There's no rush. Oh, the card.

I almost forgot the card.

Thirty decagrams of meat.

Well, we'll see.

Every morning she goes to the market and gets in line. In the second year of the war, when she was still new in Vienna and there wasn't yet a vegetable shortage, she liked to finger the carrots, potatoes, or cabbage, just like back home.

Hands off the merchandise! the Viennese shouted at her, sometimes even slapping her hand away as if she were a disobedient child.

Surely it isn't forbidden to look a bit before one buys.

Look all you like, but no pawing.

Later they simply pushed her away when she wanted to touch something intended for her stomach. *Fire, locusts, leeches, plague, bears, foxes, snakes, insects, lice.* But did these people ever stop to think about what it really meant to introduce things growing in the world into their bodies?

No matter. *Zol es brennen*, to hell with it.

Meanwhile, most of the sellers had armed themselves against these Galician refugees and their barbaric ways by posting signs: *Touching the merchandise is strictly prohibited.*

If only there were still merchandise left.

In her own shop back home, if she had forbidden the customers to touch her wares, she'd have gone out of business right away. When she thinks of all she left behind when she fled—the eggs, the sacks full of flour and sugar, the barrels of herring, all the apples—she could weep. People here are insolent, and they won't even give you what you are entitled to according to your ration card. When she stands in line unsuccessfully, she sometimes gathers up a few cabbage leaves, rotten potatoes, or whatever else may have fallen into the snow around the vegetable sellers' stands, and puts them in her bag.

That's still perfectly good. What are they thinking? They're experts at throwing things away, these goyim.

9

At the end of January her friend suddenly falls desperately ill. Lying in bed with a fever of 104°, she keeps talking about a pit filled with human flesh and a small child standing beside the pit who wants to gobble up all the meat. Her friend's fiancé doesn't know what to do; together they carry the sick woman down the stairs and bring her in a taxi to the barracks that was set up the year before in the General Hospital's courtyard to accommodate those stricken by the epidemic. The next day they are not allowed in to see her, nor the day after that, and what's more, a pulmonary infection has now made her illness worse, they're told; on the fourth day they learn that the patient's situation is very grave indeed, and on the fifth the doctor informs them that her friend died of the Spanish flu that very morning, at 3:20 a.m.

What's going to happen to her now? her fiancé asks.

The 7031 will come for her tonight around eleven, the doctor says.

Who?

You must have been away at war a long time if you've never heard of it.

Yes, the fiancé says.

Explain it to him, the doctor says to her and leaves.

We're going to stay here and wait, she says.

For what?

For the 7031.

They remain standing there until after nightfall, leaning against the wall of the hospital building, above their heads are two endless rows of windows, but no one is looking out to where they stand down below: everyone behind these windows is asleep or terminally ill, no one can get up and look out—the dead windows retreat before their eyes in two rows, growing narrower as they recede, impenetrably sealed. The arc lamps illuminate the street only until ten in the evening, after this it is completely dark. Every once in a while, one of them crouches, or walks a few steps. The fiancé smokes until his jacket pockets are empty. When it begins to snow, the two take shelter beneath the archway that four days ago was an entryway and soon will be an exit. *Healing and Comfort for the Sick* is written on a plaque above the arch. And then, shortly before midnight, the streetcar bearing the number 7031 really does arrive with its twelve horizontal slots for the dead, custom built the year before (when the horse carts could no longer keep pace with the city's mortality rate). There is a silent loading up of several coffins—their mutual friend is silently lying in one of them—no one is standing on the running board of the car to catch a bit of air, and the end of the car, which used to contain doors for the living, has been nailed shut by the New Viennese Tramway Society. The two mourners are left behind in Alserstrasse, and their leave-taking from their friend is the silent, electrically operated driving off of streetcar number 7031. Above the conductor—who doesn't even glance at the bereaved because he is busy operating the starting lever and making sure the switches for the rails are correctly set—an illuminated sign displays the car's destination: Gate IV, Central Cemetery, Vienna.

10

The tremors were regular and soundless; they consisted of a slow swaying motion whose direction (judging by pictures set in motion on the wall), was north to south. Isolated small cracks are reported to have appeared on ceilings. As life continued, his wife's manner—which at first he had found charming, a sort of childish stubbornness—solidified and became something different. This metamorphosis took place in stages, but the exact point when what might be described as severity began to dominate is something he can, in retrospect, no longer say.

Early on in their marriage, she had sometimes asked him to extend his lunch hour, so that after they ate they would still have time to take a walk—oh, just blow off the office, she'd say, making a blowing sound—or when they read *Faust* together, dividing up the roles, she would want him to read Gretchen's lines, and once, to please her, he'd had to put on his dress uniform, when no one but she and the children was there to see it. Her requests had been laughable, they'd both laughed at them; fulfilling one of these requests had been simple enough, but it was also simple to say no to her and laugh all the same.

Together with the child's grandmother, they had decided that half a year after their marriage—for which he'd had to declare himself unaffiliated with any faith—he would officially return to the Catholic church, just as—together with the child's grandmother—they'd decided to baptize the child on its first birthday. Even so, as far as he could remember, they had their first argument over why she, the child's mother, shouldn't have her name entered into the baptismal registry, not even with the supplement *Israelite*. After all, if it weren't for her, the child wouldn't even be alive! He hadn't been able to think of any way to save the child. And it had turned out that all that was needed was a handful of snow, nothing more than that!

Her bringing up the handful of snow disconcerted him.

The baptism wasn't my idea in the first place, he said, it was your mother's.

So then marry my mother!

To this he gave no response.

Money is what she gives me. Money, she said.

Surely there are worse things than a mother giving her daughter money.

Money, she said once more with contempt in her voice, but then she fell silent. He never learned what she'd have wanted from her mother in place of the money.

For years they depended on the money they accepted from her mother, just to pay the rent; but when their second child came along, they couldn't afford a maid or nanny, and there came a point when they could no longer even afford to buy tickets when traveling theater companies came to town.

One thing his wife realized long ago was that she couldn't re-proach him for his failure to rise through the ranks. She had to swal-low her vexation, mulling it over in silence, and was increasingly to be found in a sour mood, impatient with the girls and with him.

The impression was that of a heavily laden cart driving rapidly across the rooftops, and only after this was a wavelike motion of the earth perceptible. There were even tremors high up in the mountains. The livestock in their alpine pastures stopped grazing, looking up with curiosity and unease. The merry little calves began leaping around.

Why did he just drop his coat instead of putting it on the hanger? Why did their older daughter quarrel with the younger one, in-stead of playing with her, why did the little one always start wail-ing like that when she bumped herself, why didn't he go down to the cellar for firewood when he saw that more was needed, why didn't he bring the clock to be repaired, or do something about the lost key? If he insisted on taking the girls to church every Sunday, why didn't he come straight home for lunch afterward instead of strolling around with them? You forget that I've spent the entire morning standing in the kitchen cooking!

A piece of glass fell from a lamp's cracked chimney, and an umbrella hang-ing from a nail fell to the floor. Whitewash fell from the ceiling of the church.

For a brief time he had nurtured the hope that by moving to Vienna they would all be moving to an easier life, but then there'd been four years of war, a capitulation, and four months of hunger, and now all their provisions—their supplies of wood, groceries, hope—were running out, the emptiness in the pantry and store-room equally great, the dirt floor showing through. Here in Vi-enna, his wife was reproaching him for one last thing: having mar-ried her, a Jewish vixen from the provinces, and not even a rich one at that. Something he had always refused to believe was apparently proving true after all: she was trapped in her Mosaic origins as if in a cage, knocking herself black and blue against its bars.

11

Perhaps her father hadn't gotten farther than Vienna when he abandoned his family. Perhaps she would run into him here at the market one day, and he would say: So there you are. When, as a little girl, she had tried to imagine where her father might be instead of with his family, she had always visualized someone who had hanged himself. Father might be in America, her mother had said. Or in France. Not that she'd believed her. But maybe her father really was right here in Vienna after all. Sometimes she forgets she was still an infant when he left. Even if he were to suddenly come walking down the street toward her, he wouldn't be able to recognize her. Sometimes she asks herself how many people walk past each other in a big city like this without even dreaming that they might actually be related to one another. Sometimes she does, in fact, run into her mother at the market, and then they exchange a few words.

Well, child, how are you and the family?

Good.

Do you have enough to eat?

Yes.

Ever since her mother came to Vienna—supposedly because she was afraid of the war—that's all her daughter feels like saying. There comes a time when a daughter should reply to her mother's question as to how she is doing with only a simple: good.

They say an aid shipment just came in from Switzerland: 1500 tons of flour, the mother says.

Well, we'll see, won't we.

Your cousin's helping you out with coal?

Uh-huh.

There comes a time when a mother should reply to her daughter's question as to how she is doing with only a simple: good. Two years ago, this cousin brought the old woman with him when he fled to Vienna, he and his wife opened a shop for pipes, paper, and toys. Sometimes her mother helped out in their shop and received a potato, a bit of offal, a small piece of cornbread in return.

How are the girls?

Good.

When she herself was still a child and perhaps really might have needed her mother, her mother had driven off in her cart every day to the farms, leaving her with her grandparents. There was no father to look after her. Her grandmother had taught her to walk—she'd learned that from her grandmother when she went to say goodbye to her before leaving for Vienna. *You took your very first steps between our crooked mud walls, and now you can go so much farther— all the way to Vienna*, her grandmother had said. But no sooner had her grandmother died than her mother followed her to Vienna, and supposedly it was because the war frightened her.

Well then.

All right.

The moment when the old woman might tell her daughter about how the Poles had beaten her husband to death would never come.

You never—you never realize . . . , the mother says.

Realize what?

You never realize how fast the time goes.

Uh-huh.

Her mother had never really spoken to her about where her father might be. Possibly he was in America, possibly in France. Her father must have had his reasons for leaving his wife so early on.

All right.

Be well, child.

The goy is fine, but now her daughter has been left hanging between two worlds, dangling, flailing, she has no choice but to brace her feet against her mother, pushing herself away from her—her mother, whose features as she ages are now so clearly marked as

81

belonging to the race of David that she is often harassed on the street, skipped over at the soup kitchen, and insulted by her neighbors.

You, too.

If her mother hadn't married her to a goy, she wouldn't be someone's mistake for her entire adult life.

12

Touching the merchandise is strictly prohibited.

The future is not lowering its prices, certainly not in times like these; but you can only buy it with the past. Lot's wife, who was too weak to leave her homeland without a final glance, who turned back knowing that the place she would see was destined for destruction, was turned into a woman of salt. This daughter is smarter. When her mother came to join her in Vienna as a refugee the first year of the war, she had kept her in her own apartment for only a few days and then as quickly as possible found one for her far enough away from her own. *How lovely is your dwelling place, oh Lord of Hosts.* Her daughters were being given a Christian upbringing and weren't sent to visit their grandmother even once. The forest provides wood for the axe that will chop it down. Each living being exhausts its own resources for those who will come after, that's what growth is. The old woman made her daughter the gift of a path leading away from her. At the moment, this path appears to be destroying her child, but it's quite possible that her granddaughters will reach the goal. Some are destined to stay behind, some to depart, and yet others to arrive.

That's how life works.

Fifteen hundred tons of flour from Switzerland, the mother said.

Well, we'll see.

13

They returned from Alserstrasse to the apartment on foot, and now they are waiting for time to pass—all at once it's become so slow. He sits beside her in the kitchen, bent over, his elbows propped on his knees, gazing at the floor in silence. Only when she hears the regular dripping does she look at him and see that tears are running down his cheeks to the tip of his nose, collecting there, and dripping to the floor tiles at his feet. Then she wants to go home. And then he says she should stay. What, stay? Stay overnight with him—who is now alone? He grabs her by the shoulders and weeps into the crook of her neck, or was it really a kiss? What? Happiness cuts shame, shame covers unhappiness, unhappiness unfurls happiness. Hope pushes aside grief, proving to be so much stronger—so strong that it surprises even the seventeen-year-old herself, this is the intensity of women fighting over bread in front of the Anker bakery—the old ones are often stronger than the younger ones, though they are so much closer to dying. Suddenly alert with hopefulness, she says: Yes, and follows the man, not heading for the vestibule this time, as she's always done when spending the night here, but instead lying down next to him at his request, obediently lying down in the bed of her friend, lying for the first time beside the man whom she has loved ever since he returned home from the war that past December like someone she'd never seen before. What? She lies down in the place of her dearest friend, who has been dead only since the morning, 3:20 a.m. The end of a day on which a life has ended is still far from being the end of days. Inconsolable, she will now—what?—inherit what belonged to her friend, who yesterday was still warm; she will metamorphose into her friend and continue her conversations in her body with their beloved. Has anyone before seen such soft lips on a man who was forced to kill so as not to be killed himself, has anyone seen such shiny, wetly gleaming teeth, and a nose whose nostrils flare with arousal, has anyone seen such long lashes shading a pair of eyes—such beautiful shadows—these lashes brought home unsinged from all the fires? Ever since the moment when he was standing there unexpectedly at the door, she has known that this is the man who was destined for her all along, and now at long last he knows it too, at long last he is lying beside her just as she imagined countless times, breathing so close beside her that she can inhale his breath, and if it weren't so dark, she would surely be able to see him gazing at her through the night, gazing all the way through her. What?

14

In the local scythe factory—situated not on the Judenburg Terrace but directly on the left bank of the Mur—fifteen cm. lengths of stacked steel were thrown in a northeasterly direction. In a smithy in Purbachgraben, approximately one hundred m. from the right bank of the Mur—where the limestone massif of the Liechtenstein Mountain descends to the Judenburg Terrace—tools on the west wall were thrown to the east. In Aichdorf a small bell tolled (plane of oscillation: east/west). In Fohnsdorf, a man was thrown out of bed in an eastwardly direction. Several persons staggered or fell in an eastwardly direction, e.g., a schoolboy on the road between Rikersdorf and Allerheiligen, who simultaneously heard a howling sound and a thunder-like crash; a local apprentice on a ladder; and in the building next door, a schoolboy on the stairs. Taking into account the objects' inertia, these findings correlate well with the observations of several witnesses, who were sitting quietly at the time and had the impression that the main thrust came from the east.

15

When her mother comes to relieve her at midnight, the younger daughter doesn't say that she just saw her older sister with a man. The two of them walked right past her where she stood hidden among the crowd of people. And she, the little sister, didn't dare call out her sister's name, her sister was walking with her head down, tight-lipped, not speaking to the man who was walking at her side. So this is how her sister spends the nights she's not at home. Years ago, when the younger sister had stumbled across her older sister's diary and read a little bit of it, her sister had suddenly come into the room, but she hadn't shouted or struck her sister when she saw what she was doing, she just calmly removed the book from her hands and said to her:

Do you think I was happy when you were born?

Maybe.

Do you remember the glass marbles you always played with?

Yes.

Do you remember the time I told you to try swallowing them?

Maybe.

Why do you think I wanted you to do that?

Dunno.

Do you remember the wall behind the house where Simon the coachman lives?

Yes.

Do you remember the time I told you to try jumping down from it?

Maybe.

Why do you think I would have said that?

Dunno.

If you ever touch this book again, you will no longer be my sister. Do you understand?

Yes.

And so now her tight-lipped sister had walked down the street beside a tight-lipped man without realizing her little sister had seen her. Even a public place like this, even in the middle of the night, could reveal something that was none of anyone else's business, just like an open book, in a city as large as Vienna there was no avoiding someone's reading it. She had been standing there for the past five hours so that her sister would be able to eat cow udder the next day in order to survive, and also so that she herself would be able to eat it to survive, along with her mother and father. Her sister, in turn, while she, the little sister, was at school, would accompany her mother to the Vienna Woods to collect firewood, for hours she and their mother would march through the frigid woods and exhaust themselves lugging armfuls of filthy waterlogged sticks, only so that the younger sister—and she herself, of course, and their mother and father—would not freeze in their own home. Nonetheless, it was perfectly possible that if this very same sister knew that her younger sister had watched her walking through the nocturnal Viennese streets at the side of a man, she would wish her dead, perhaps with more success this time. How many fronts like these were there in a life that might cost a person her life? How arduous it was surviving all the battles in which one would not fall.

16

But then, the man falls asleep as soon as he is lying beside her, the warmth of his body next to the warmth of her body, the man does not touch her the entire night, not even in a dream. All night long she hears him breathing next to her; from breath to breath, she knows with increasing certainty there is no point putting out a hand to touch him. The weeping that has been stuck in her throat ever since the departure of the 7031 now breaks to the surface, but now they are tears of a different sort: This weeping for her dead friend gets twisted—still in her throat—into a weeping out of jealousy, tears of mourning become tears of fury at the man she loves, who has invited her to share his bed but now is refusing to console her for the loss he has suffered. By the end of the night, she is weeping only out of shame. She has now received an answer once and for all to a question that, left to her own devices, she would not have asked for a long time, perhaps never. An answer she would never willingly have asked for, namely that the man is friendly but does not love her, that his mourning for the deceased is genuine and deep, while her own duplicitous nature has no counterpart anywhere in the world. If he shared her sentiments, how little would she care what her father, mother, and friends had to say about it, but now this defeat has condemned her irrevocably. Sleeping, he had encouraged her to hope, and sleeping, he has struck her down in crushing defeat. Lonelier than ever, she arises at dawn from the side of the sleeping man; no one who knew what she had hoped for could ever wish to consort with her again; she herself has no choice but to go on enduring her body, which has led her so badly astray, if only she had gone home the night before, as she'd originally intended, the way home would have been nothing more than walking, setting one foot before the other. But now she knows what it means to no longer have any possibility of retreat. She gathers up her things and leaves the apartment without waking him.

17

At some point, nearly morning, she finally ... what time though, dunno, around six or maybe seven? Dunno. Was she crying? I don't think so. I was just surprised when she refused to get up, even at nine she was still, she didn't get up all morning, her eyes were shut, but she wasn't sleeping. And not a bite of anything. Not even coffee.

All day long just lying there. I'm going to lie here and never get up again, she said to me. Really. She wouldn't come to the woods on Tuesday either. No one on earth. On Wednesday I got the eggs from Mizzi but she didn't want hers. And then the night after, her hair! Exactly, I didn't go out for my chess game; I really thought we'd be off to Steinhof to commit her. So did I. Her beautiful hair. But on Friday she seemed better. Yes, that was my impression too. Completely calm. There was a fresh snowfall on Saturday, her first time downstairs. I draped my coat over her, and downstairs she said it made her dizzy to look at the falling snow. I said: so don't look. And I said: eat something proper, then you'll be able to stand on your feet again. And she opened her mouth and let the snowflakes fall into it. Yes, that's right. I couldn't help laughing. Me neither.

And then it was Sunday.

18

On Sunday, thank God, the older girl finally wants to go out for a little walk again. Are you going to see your friend? her mother asks. Yes, she says. Her mother shuts the door behind her; before the door closes, the girl hears her mother calling to her father: Don't you think it's strange that her friend didn't come to see her even once? Well, how could she? Maybe on the 7031? It's her parents' own fault they know so little about their daughter. It's not as if anyone ever asked her if she wanted a sister in the first place, or whether she liked Vienna so much the first time they visited that she wanted to move there. When a handicrafts teacher at the lyceum had used the words *sloppy* and *shoddy* to describe a doll's dress she had sewn with great effort, she'd understood that even after years in Vienna she was still a foreigner here and would remain one. She still remembers her grandmother coming to stay with them right after she fled Galicia; for several days the kitchen had smelled like in the old days, smelled of pear compote and challah, but when the provisions her grandmother had brought with her were exhausted, her mother had immediately found the old woman another apartment and forbidden her daughters to visit her there. *How lovely is your dwelling place, oh Lord of Hosts.* Only then did she realize that she, too, was of Jewish descent, but her father still took her and her sister to services at a Christian church Sunday after Sunday, they sat in the civil servants' pew with other civil servants and their families. For more than ten years now, her father had been telling his colleagues that his wife wasn't so steady on her feet and therefore attended a church closer to their home, and in this way—this much one must grant him—he had advanced to the ninth pay grade, but even for a civil servant of that grade, it was no great feat these days to starve to death as miserably as the monkeys, camels, and donkeys in the Schönbrunn Menagerie. Did keeping her misguided love a secret from her friend make her just as halfhearted and deceitful as her parents? It had done no good to keep the truth to herself either, for a truth remained even if it was never spoken aloud, day after day it went on doing what it had to. Landstrasser Hauptstrasse, Arenbergpark, Neulinggasse— which eventually turns into Gusshausstrasse on the way to the district called Margareten and then later becomes Schleifmühlgasse— and finally Margaretenstrasse itself—the scrap of paper on which her mother had written down her grandmother's address had been right there in the kitchen drawer.

19

Time to go. Let's go.

Every Sunday she went to the Vienna Woods to get firewood. She would take the tram to the end of the line at Rodaun or Hacking, along with a great many others. Like her, they would carry baskets, rucksacks, or satchels on their backs; from there, she'd enter the woods to collect kindling, perhaps breaking off a branch here and there that was not too heavy.

My cousin helping me out with coal—wouldn't that be nice. Hat, coat, glove. Good.

Returning home in the evening, she sometimes had to let a tram or two pass before managing to squeeze into one of the overcrowded cars, so she often remained standing at the tram stop in the dark for over an hour, freezing, while in the illuminated tram people stood or sat, with the wood they had gathered sprouting awkwardly from their rucksacks and panniers.

And the basket. And the rucksack.

From the outside, a tram like that resembled an aquarium, and when the car lurched into motion or braked, all the people behind the fogged-up glass swayed back and forth with their bundles of twigs like one huge organism.

Oh, it's all getting tangled up. What a disaster. The boots. Now look, it's falling out the top. Oh, this shvakhkeyt, *this weakness. Well.*

Even before this, she'd thought at times that deprivation made people more alike, made their movements, down to the gestures of their hands and fingers, ever more predictable. When she encountered other people in the woods who were also looking for wood, she saw their bending over, their breaking twigs, their stripping off the dry leaves—exactly resembling her own bending, breaking, and stripping. When it came down to surviving the hunger and cold, and nothing more, all human beings adopted this same economy of movement, perhaps still common to them from back when they were animals, while everything that distinguished them from each other was suddenly recognizable as a luxury.

All right, that's good now. Oh, I almost forgot the key. That would have been something.

20

You just have to start walking, then a street name scrawled on a scrap of paper with a building and apartment number will turn into a route to follow: with buildings on either side, with weather (cold and damp), with the sound of footsteps sinking into slush and snow, and with other people on this or that errand, willing or unwilling; a route that leads you past dimly lit taverns and shops whose windows are almost empty or sealed up with shutters. The low, stooped building where the old woman lives has a stone angel keeping watch over the entryway. *How lovely is your dwelling place, oh Lord of Hosts.* After fleeing the provinces and spending her first few days in Vienna in her daughter's apartment, the old woman told her older granddaughter about the two angels that prophesied the fall of Sodom to Lot and conducted him to safety. These angels were so beautiful that the citizens of Sodom wanted nothing more than to tear the flesh from their limbs and devour them. *Sheyn vi di zibn veltn.* As beautiful as the seven worlds. Now, as the older granddaughter presses down on the door handle, trying to remember how her grandmother said this sentence to her, it suddenly seems unfamiliar, and she wonders whether she just dreamed it.... *As beautiful.* The building's dark entryway stinks, above one of the doors on the ground floor is a little metal plate with the apartment number. In the stairwell, it seems that some of the windows facing the courtyard are broken and have been replaced with wooden panels. The beautiful man; oh, his lips, the wings of his nose, his eyelashes. Has beauty never had any other purpose than to cause those who wish to possess it to rise up against each other, and, in the end, between them, tear the beautiful object to shreds, or, failing that, destroy each other instead? She rings the bell and also knocks on the door, but no one answers. As a girl, she had marched to the *Rathaus*, demanding that the war come to an end. Now she is in the middle of her own war, one in which—even at so great a distance from bombs, grenades and poison gas—she is still finding it infinitely difficult to survive each day from beginning to end, and then all through the night.

21

What in the Lord God's name did we do on Sunday evening?

Of the fourteen persons who fell victim to lightning in 1898, two were killed by lighting bolts striking inside buildings, two under trees, one under a wayside shrine where he'd taken cover, and seven out in the open, including two reapers working in the fields. In two cases, I was unable to determine the precise circumstances. Outside the town of Laufen an der Sann, lightning struck a woman who was carrying a hoe on her back. The woman was paralyzed, and a mark was left behind on her back in the shape of the hoe.

After the older girl went out on Sunday evening, her mother threaded new shoelaces in her younger daughter's shoes. After the older girl went out on Sunday evening, her father spread out his files on the kitchen table and started reading. On Sunday evening, after her older sister had gone out, the younger girl did her mathematics homework, her mother got her sewing kit from the cold parlor and began to darn socks, and her father experimented with whether he could read better with his glasses on or without, he pushed the glasses down and looked over the top of them, then pushed them back up and finally said: This typeface really isn't easy to read. The younger girl then put more wood on the fire, and the wood hissed because it was so damp. Her mother said: Go wash your hands, otherwise you'll make your notebook dirty. The younger girl washed her hands in the bucket. The mother bit off the thread. The father turned the page of the file. The younger girl wiped her hands on her dress, sitting back down at the table. Her mother looked for a different color of thread in her sewing basket. Her father laid his glasses to one side and went on reading. The young girl dipped her pen into the inkwell and solved her arithmetic problem. Her mother coughed. Her father turned over another page of the file.

22

Margaretenstrasse, Heumühlgasse (down one or the other of those streets), then Rechte Wienzeile, across the Naschmarkt, Linke Wienzeile, somewhere or other, Girardigasse, Gumpendorfer Strasse, Stiegengasse, Windmühlgasse; everywhere, the snow is piled up shoulder-height on either side—Theobaldgasse, Rahlgasse—just as high on the right as on the left—Mariahilfer Strasse, Babenberger Strasse, Opernring—and it's slippery, as smooth as glass. Does she really want to turn onto Opernring? Or would it be better to take a left onto Burgring? Today, it is exactly one week since she waited on Alserstrasse with the man she loves for the 7031. How long does a week last? Crossing the street to the left, toward the Museum of Fine Arts, would mean picking her way between two gigantic heaps of snow with a frozen puddle in between, so she turns to the right. In the opera house on the other side of the street, music and listening to music are locked up together. Why is she walking around outside? To exhaust herself to the point where she can neither see nor hear? Is she indulging in a stroll? Strolling to her demise? Two pounds of butter, someone whispers at her cold back. How much? She keeps going. Two pounds of butter and fifty decagrams of veal. The man's whisperings insinuate themselves beneath the broad brim of her hat, slipping into her ear from behind. Two pounds of butter, fifty decagrams of veal, ten candles. Although the entire world lies open before her, which she thought might put an end to her hearing, she can hear what the man is offering in exchange for her person. Is she interested? Or would she rather return home, where what is called her life is taking place: her father reading his files, her little sister doing her homework, her mother calling her, her older daughter, a whore. *Salome* is being performed tonight. How long has it been since her parents went out together? Does she know a good reason not to accept? Or is she not so sure? When she turns around, she sees a young man, perhaps only slightly older than she is; he has no hat on, even though it's the middle of winter, so she sees his thin hair, by the time he's twenty-five he'll have a bald spot, she thinks, and she's surprised to see beads of sweat on his forehead in the middle of winter.

Two pounds of butter, he repeats, looking at her, fifty decagrams of veal, ten candles.

He says her price right to her face.

And why not twelve candles, she says and starts to laugh.

The time when it went without saying that the freshly fallen snow would promptly be carted from the streets of the Viennese city center to the Danube and dumped into the channel that had been knocked clear of ice is long past. Thanks to the war, something is missing: men, the freshly fallen men. The most that happens now is that the snow gets pushed aside, shoveled into heaps by a couple of war invalids, women and children; on warmer days these heaps of snow begin to melt until they are ringed with puddles that freeze over during the night in precisely those spots where the path was to remain clear. The layer of ice covering the sidewalks of Vienna, in heavily traveled spots above all, has grown so hard and thick in the course of the winter that no one even tries to chop it up any longer. Pedestrians wishing to cross from Babenberger Strasse to the Museum of Fine Arts or to walk down Burgring on the left away from the city center must take particular care not to fall. Captain Eduard Gabler, for instance, suffered a compound fracture of his forearm just yesterday when he fell on the ice walking at Freud-enauer Winterhafen; Private Franz Adler also broke his forearm, on Marxergasse; factory owner Mortiz Gerthofer suffered an exposed fracture of his right shin on Nobilegasse; and nurse Frieda Bertin fell on Mariahilfer Strasse, not at all far from here, suffering a severe contusion of the left hip. Where one crosses Babenberger Strasse toward the Art History Museum, away from the city center, the ice between two heaps of snow has long since been polished smooth by the heavy pedestrian traffic, even though yesterday's snowfall briefly covered it up. But because of the countless shoes, and also several bare feet, that have passed over this spot since then, the snow has become inseparably conjoined with the ice over the course of the morning, itself becoming ice. This ice appears black—though of course there is no deep body of water beneath its surface—and it displays the approximate contours of the African continent on a smaller scale. Seamstress Cilli Bujanow nearly slipped on this bit of ice around 2:30 in the afternoon, but was propped up by Lieu-tenant Colonel of the Chamber of Finances Alfred Kern, who happened to be walking behind her, sparing her the fall. Seven-year-old Leopoldine Thaler practiced skating on the puddle as she passed, eleven-year-old pupil David Robitschek attempted to shat-ter the ice by jumping up and down on it (unsuccessful), a stray dog of unknown provenance urinated on the right-hand heap of snow, causing a portion of the ice, corresponding roughly to the region of former German East Africa, to melt and also dyeing the area yellow approximately as far down as the Niger. By six, this bit too has frozen again, although the surface of the ice in this area is slightly roughened. The young lady who at approximately 6:00 p.m. at first considers crossing Babenberger Strasse here and then walking to the left toward of the Museum of Fine Arts would be compelled—before reaching the rougher area north of the Equa-tor that promises salvation in the form of a firm foothold—to step on the treacherously slippery territory of South Africa, but at the last minute, she loses her nerve, and instead heads off to the right in the direction of Opernring.

So you aren't one after all, the pale lad asks long after she has stopped laughing. No, she says. She's surprised at how hard the young man is sweating even though he doesn't have his coat buttoned. She wouldn't mind being cheap if it meant she wouldn't be on her own forever with all the time in the world. How many people can simultaneously be in possession of all the time in the world? Would she like to ...? She decides to join him for a glass of wine. That is ... She has no idea how grateful ... In the café he seizes her hands and holds them to his face, using them to wipe the tears from his eyes and the mucus from his nose, perhaps she'll excuse him, he's never been with one before, but just now he wanted, perhaps she will understand, you see his fiancée just, that is, no longer, and sent him packing, although for two years now, an engagement after all, or doesn't that mean ...

How long does a life last, anyhow?

Seventy or eighty years?

Doesn't she already know more than she can bear?

... his fiancée would see all right if he carried on just like she did, preferably with lots of girls ... really, though, someone ought to kill her.

Oh dear, the young woman thinks, her hands already dripping with tears. Does he know her, this man? Does he know what she has wished for? Does he know what a burden she is finding life, which from inside always looked to her like a sphere with perfectly smooth, black walls, and you keep running and running and there isn't even a shabby little door to let you out?

He'd have shot her if only she'd come out of her building, he says. But she knew what he was capable of, so she stayed where she was, and what was he supposed to do now ... he never thought ... after all he was ... and he'd always treated her ... and never once ... He'd have shot her? she asked. How?

96

Right here, he says, slipping his fingers into the right-hand pocket of his coat, it's my father's Mauser.

Now all at once she understands why she is sitting here with this man, on whose face what goes by the name of heartache—in her own case, too—makes so pitiful an impression. Now the inside of the sphere that always seemed infinite to her suddenly contains this shabby little door. You know what, she says, pulling her hands away from the sobbing man, it would be the easiest thing in the world to insult your fiancée in a way she will remember all her life. Really? he says, looking up, and meanwhile she is drying off her hands on her skirt under the table.

Her mother says: I'm going to bed now, she gathers up her sewing things, puts them back in their basket, brings the basket back out to the cold parlor. Her father calls: I'm coming, too. Her sister has already been lying in bed for half an hour, but despite the darkness she's still awake. Her father picks up the carbide lamp by its handle.

Do you really think? he says.

Of course.

And if something goes wrong?

They'll certainly know what to do on Alserstrasse if anything goes wrong.

Healing and Comfort for the Sick.

And if everything goes right, she thinks, we'll soon enough be continuing our journey on the quietest car of the New Viennese Tramway Society.

All right, I'm going to call her and tell her.

But just one sentence.

Just one sentence.

He settles up, she says goodbye to the waiter, that's how easy it is to pass from one world to the next. The telephone booth is just across the street, and when the youth puts his weight on the floor of the booth, the light goes on—a soul would be telephoning in the dark, she thinks. Just one sentence. She waits outside in the snow, watching the lovesick young man speaking in the light: he speaks, listens, responds again, listens, contradicts. She'd better drag him back out of this cell, otherwise he might slide back over to the other side again; the glass panes of the booth are already fogging up with his hot breath when she pulls open the door.

In the receiver a female voice is exclaiming: For the love of God, speak with my daughter tomorrow!

Tomorrow will be too late!

But I'm telling you she isn't here!

Please tell her that even in death I was—

You still have your whole life ahead of you!

Now he falls silent. He says nothing at all. His hair is thin, at twenty-five, he might already have a bald spot. Then she calmly takes the receiver from his hand, and in his place she says into it:

Don't you understand? He has to die.

We have to go stand in line at five o'clock. . . . You don't always have to be looking men in the face like that. . . . I have to do all the work myself. . . . Your grandmother has to take responsibility for herself.

And the young man?

He's got to die now, that's all there is to it, and she has to ride in his sled with him, all the way to hell.

She says the one thing and only thinks the rest, then she hangs up the telephone.

The mother hears the father shutting the kitchen door so that the warmth from the stove will keep until morning, then he goes out to the stairs, the toilet is half a flight down. It flushes with water from the tap in the hall. The mother turns over on her other side. The older girl has only just gotten back on her feet again, and already it's anyone's guess what she's up to. She sacrificed herself for this daughter, who almost died as a baby, and this is the thanks she gets.

The younger daughter doesn't like it when her sister's bed stays empty overnight. If her sister were to move out altogether, as she sometimes threatens when she's fighting with their mother, there'd be just one advantage: they'd stop referring to her, the younger sister, as the little one. The teacher said on Friday that Austria is now only one-tenth its original size. She, on the other hand, has grown during the war years, she's now five foot seven. So the borders of the country she lives in have nothing at all to do with her own size, but it's probably best if she doesn't point this out in class tomorrow.

The father turns out the light and lies down in the dark bed beside the mother. The blue-tinged shadows around the chin of his older daughter these past few weeks involuntarily remind him of something he doesn't want to be reminded of, but his thoughts don't much care whether or not he wishes to think them; when the time is right they make their way, like it or not, through the thicket of all the things he has ever thought or seen.

And now here they are in front of the opera house, Salome has already been served Jochanaan's head on a silver platter, the bloody papier-mâché head with wool hair that is now back in its place in the dark properties closet, on the shelf beside the wooden platter someone painted silver. They have agreed to take a taxi to Alserstrasse. They will isolate the precise moment when the taxi stops in front of the hospital and remove it forever from amid all the other time that exists. The taxi drives up Burgring, takes a left onto Volksgartenstrasse, then heads north up the avenue known first as Museumsstrasse, then Auerspergstrasse and finally Landesgerichtsstrasse where Alserstrasse turns off to the left. The trip takes no longer than five and a half minutes, during which not a word is spoken in the back seat of the taxi. In front of the entrance to the hospital the taxi driver stops, just as his passengers requested.

23

Action for the Victims of the Three Nights of Blood in Lemberg: Hermine and Ignaz Klinger, 100 crowns; in remembrance of my beloved mother Terka Korsky, 120 crowns; Frau Kamler, 10 crowns; in total 230 crowns. This is printed on the piece of newspaper the old woman is rolling up to light the fire. She had the right idea. Starting with the goy for her daughter, then the train ticket she gave the young family for their trip to Vienna to see the Corpus Christi procession, and then her own flight. The sticks from the Vienna Woods are covered with lichen that produces foul-smelling fumes when burned. Nights of blood. Andrei. The nursemaid who refused to open the door for her and her husband. The Almighty took her husband's life instead of the life of their daughter.

Where could Father be?

In America, or France.

Don't you care?

Only God can know where he is. Go wash your hands.

Let her daughter go on thinking that for some reason or other she was incapable of holding onto the girl's father. She had held onto him, held him to the end, when he was nothing more than a bit of flesh. But should she have said that to her daughter, should she have told her that she too, the mother, had also been in danger of becoming nothing more than a bit of flesh, and the daughter, too, and that under similar circumstances the daughter's own girls—the big one and the little one—might themselves be only flesh? For someone who didn't know, did it make a difference whether a person was dead or just very far away? The murderers' guilt now looked like her own guilt, but was that important? In Lemberg not long ago the Poles celebrated their victory over the Ukranians on the main square, while two blocks away the Jewish quarter was set on fire. They celebrated for three nights. Jewish children who tried to run away were tossed back into the burning buildings by the legion-naires, but on the other side of the barricades there was accordion music. *Es vert mir finster in di oygn*, everything's going black before my eyes. In Vienna she doesn't have much company, but she is alive. Her daughter is alive, and so are the two girls.

24

Redhead, redhead, ding-a-ling, fire burns in Wahring, fire burns in Ottakring, you're a nice smoked herring! That the promises were not kept. That no one who asks wants to hear the answer. That her own interior would have always remained an exterior, even with her tongue inside another during a kiss. To dissolve the borders, that's all she wanted. Why was it not possible for her to love her friend and also her friend's beloved; what exactly was being forbidden her, and by whom? Why was she not permitted to plunge into love as into a river, and why, if she was being forbidden to swim in these waters, was there no one else swimming there? Why did her mother call her a whore? Why wasn't she allowed to tell anyone that her grandmother was Jewish? Was there really so little love in the world that it wasn't enough to glue things together? Why were there differences, why this hierarchy of worth? Or was it only her own deficiencies making everything fall apart? In any case, it was high time for her to subtract herself from the world.

The Mauser C96 is a weapon that was not regularly used during the First World War but nonetheless enjoyed great popularity. The special feature of the C96 is that the magazine is located not within the weapon's grip but in front of the trigger. On Sunday, January 26, 1919, at approximately 11:17 p.m., seated in a taxi that has just arrived in front of Alserstrasse 4, the Vienna General Hospital,

48.21497 degrees latitude north, 16.35231 degrees longitude east, Herr Ferdinand G., a medical student in his third semester, acting in accordance with a mutual agreement, places the muzzle of this handy weapon against the temple of a young woman with whom he is only fleetingly acquainted, and at the very moment that a dog barks outside somewhere—in response to this barking, as it were— he pulls the trigger.

Finally, she doesn't have to be trapped in this skin any longer. Finally, this random individual has opened the shabby door with a gunshot, and she is released into the open air. *Healing and Comfort for the Sick.* A dead woman has infinite relatives; she is now infinitely loved and can love anyone she likes, all the while dissolving entirely, with her dead thoughts, in all the others. Did anyone ever see such soft lips on a man before? She now floats upon these lips, utterly interspersed with the one she loves, drifting far away, the two of them are the water and also the dark blue sky above it, and all who were trapped behind the two endless rows of windows have now flung them open and are breathing deeply in and out.

But then a second shot is fired, and the blood of this happenstance individual splatters on her face, someone's happenstance blood is making her hair wet, or is it her own blood? Only now does she realize her skull is exploding with pain, but why hasn't it exploded; isn't she supposed to be dead? Someone opens the door: the taxi driver holds out an arm to the one shot dead so that she can get out, cold Viennese air floods her skull, swirling past her thoughts, she has been laid bare all the way beneath her skin. For the Lord God's sake, she hears the driver say, and now she also hears the shabby Viennese weeping of this happenstance individual, who apparently was not capable of skillfully shooting her and himself as they agreed. Before her closed eyes, a treacherously slippery South Africa appears, she places her foot upon it and slips and then falls and falls and falls. *If*

102

only I had known there's no floor left once you go through the door, she thinks, and then she stops thinking, just as she imagined she would.

Her mother sleeps, her father sleeps, her sister is dreaming fitfully but is asleep as well. In a portfolio on the kitchen table, in the dark kitchen, lie her father's papers, but no one is reading them in the middle of the night, no one is wondering what happened on August 20, 1897, in Wetzelsdorf at the foot of the Buchkogel: *The birds in their cages fell down from their perches, people leapt horrified out of bed, all were seized by a general terror. At the same time a violent downpour began.* In the bedroom shared by the two girls, hidden behind the wardrobe, is a thick notebook containing the older girl's diary.

25

Just before four in the morning, the police bang on the door so loudly that the glass set into its upper half rattles; the girl's mother is the first to wake up. The following three days, her older daughter remains unconscious, and except for the rising and falling of her rib cage, she lies perfectly immobile in the hospital bed; even without moving, she is wrestling inside with death, they say. Her mother complains to the nurses that her daughter has to lie in a room with twelve beds under these conditions. Her father says: Let it be. Her mother complains about the stink and the cries of the other patients. Her father says: Listen. Her mother asks the doctor, who at one point carelessly referred to her daughter as a suicide: Don't you ever wash your hands?

Her father sits in silence beside his older daughter's deathbed.

Did you see the dirt under his fingernails?

No.

I don't want someone like that touching my child.

A man makes a coat out of an old piece of cloth.
When the coat is in tatters, he makes a vest from the coat.
When the vest is in tatters, he makes a scarf from the vest.
When the scarf is in tatters, he makes a cap from the scarf.
When the cap is in tatters, he makes a button from the cap.
From the button the man makes a nothing at all.
And then from the nothing at all he makes this song.

On Wednesday night, sometime between midnight and 1:30 a.m., between the first and second rounds the nurse makes through the twelve-bed room, the young woman finally stops breathing. An official of the Roman Catholic Archdiocese of Vienna enters the young woman's name in the large Registry of Deaths the next morning. When the younger sister stops by on her way home from school that afternoon to pay a visit, she finds an empty bed, and when she asks where her sister is, she is told that her sister has been brought downstairs to the storeroom for the dead.

26

And her murderer is still alive, her mother says, the murderer of my daughter did quite nicely for himself, and now the girl is dead.

Leave it alone, her father says, and who's saying he's even going to pull through?

Leave it alone, that's all you have to say when our child lets a person like that shoot her?

A person like what? asks their younger daughter, who will soon be known only as their daughter.

I tell you, if you start gallivanting around like your sister, I'll give you what for.

They say she hardly knew him, her father says.

So she hardly knew him—apparently it was enough to have him whack her.

The younger girl is silent. Her sister once forbade her to poke into her secrets and possibly betray them to her parents or to anyone else whose business they were not, and the prohibition is still alive and well. What good would it do now after the fact if she told her parents that she saw her sister walking through the streets of Vienna with a man on Sunday, a week and a half ago?

Until Sunday, a week and a half ago, everything was fine, her father says. True enough, says her mother.

She did, however, sometime on Monday just before dawn ... her father says ... and even on Tuesday, says the younger daughter ... no one in the world ... her father says, and on Wednesday I ... and then that night, the younger one says, exactly, on Friday it seemed as if ... her father says, on Saturday, fresh snowfall, says her father, the younger sister says: And then came Sunday....

Would you two stop, her mother says now to her husband and daughter, you're not going to bring her back with talk like that.

How awful that you never truly know what's going on, her father says.

Her mother says: Be grateful.

What in the good Lord God's name did we do on Sunday evening, her father asks and begins to cry.

27

Not until Friday afternoon—in the Pathological Institute they are investigating the path of the bullet and whether the young woman didn't perhaps shoot herself after all—does her father set off for Margareten. (Her mother says she has her hands full with all the formalities, someone's got to see to it that life goes on.) The dark entryway stinks, and above one of the doors on the ground floor is a little metal plate with the apartment number. The girl's grandmother doesn't say anything when she learns what has happened, but her entire body begins to tremble. The girl's father remembers the first time he came into her shop and saw her daughter, whose skin was so white, it would have blinded him like snow if he'd been a bug crawling around on it. He remembers that not long afterward, the shopkeeper showed him her daughter's bed, and a cat lay curled up on it asleep. He just nods to her in silence and turns to go, opening the apartment door himself and then shutting it behind him. A number of the windows that in better days used to look out on the courtyard from the stairwell have been nailed up with boards.

When the investigations have been completed on Monday, the official enters *cerebral hemorrhage* under "cause of death" in the Registry of Deaths, and on Tuesday the funeral is held in the Catholic section of Vienna's Central Cemetery, at Gate III. At the edge of the dark pit, the sacristan says a prayer, father and younger sister cross themselves, and the mother keeps her hands in her coat pockets. *Yene velt*. The world to come. The grandmother might have come to see that her granddaughter at least made it as far as the Catholic cemetery, but no doubt she prefers to keep them waiting instead. Once again she is leaving her daughter to deal with the most difficult things alone, just as in the old days, when she couldn't even teach her to walk.

Perhaps, the younger girl thinks, everything would have gone differently if she had swallowed the glass marbles as her sister commanded, jumped down from Simon's wall, or allowed her sister to cause her death in some other way. Had her sister now gone in her place? Had she not been thinking of her at all when she died? Her father takes a handful of earth and throws it into the grave. When the snow fell—the snow that is making the heap of freshly dug earth, the dark hillock stand out—his daughter was still alive.

Over there, on the other side of the high wall, is the Israelite Cemetery; no tree rises into the air there, the sky is unimpeded, someone who doesn't know better might expect there would be streetcar tracks on the other side, or open fields, but her mother knows it is on purpose no trees were planted, for if one day the roots of the trees were to go zigzagging between the remaining bones of a person buried there, prying them apart, the person would no longer be whole when his name was called for the Last Judgment.

When they return from the cemetery, their daughter eats her own portion of mutton, then she eats her father's portion, since he says he can't get it down, and finally she eats the portion belonging to her dead sister. (Her mother didn't report that they are now one person fewer, therefore she was given the twelve-and-a-half decagrams of meat due the deceased along with the rest of the family's rations when she exchanged the still-valid stamps at the Grosser Markt early that morning.) *God our Father whom we love, you gave us teeth, now give us food.* It's only now that her sister lies buried that the younger daughter is so hungry.

28

But then the cousin, who has never before come to visit, rings the bell, just to say that. Well, what? That the girl's grandmother, the very day she learned of her older granddaughter's death, fell down the cellar steps and, as he put it, landed badly, and now—well, they probably understand what he meant. So it really does look as if things won't start looking up again until they are as black as pitch. Her mother rises to her feet and starts stacking the dirty plates. When she set the table, it was in the belief that she had a mother who was still alive. Does it make a difference to someone who doesn't know the truth whether a person is dead or just very far away? The cousin says it took him several days to track down the family's address, and the funeral has already taken place as Jewish law demands. Is there still a war on, the daughter thinks, is that why so many are dying all at once? I can't imagine what she wanted in the cellar, her father says, she must have run out of coal long ago. *Ver veyst*, the cousin says, who knows. Now, the father thinks, he will have to stay alive until after the first of the month, and also the first of the next month, and the month after that, so that the dying doesn't get the upper hand, so that everything will remain balanced and not suddenly begin to tip; the father thinks this but says nothing. Gate IV, Field 3, Row 8, Plot 12, the cousin writes on a scrap of paper which, after he's left, her mother puts in the kitchen drawer.

29

In the middle of a snowy field—a few gravestones here and there—at the very back of the Israelite section of the cemetery, it would be easy to find the hillock of freshly disturbed dirt. Gate I, Gate II, Gate III and finally Gate IV. According to the beliefs a person held while alive, he or she will come to lie in the ground near either one or the other tram stop. Less than a minute and a half's ride separates deceased Protestants, Catholics, and Israelites. From her grandmother's grave, a mourner could easily glance over at the high wall surrounding the Catholic cemetery at the tall, snow-covered trees, and in this silence, even at a distance, she'd be able to hear the sound the snow makes when, having grown too heavy for its own good, it slides from a branch, making the branch spring quickly back into the air.

30

It is cold inside her dead mother's apartment, cold and dark. Even the water in the bucket is frozen. When she goes to empty it in the courtyard, it falls to the ground as a solid lump of ice. *Fire, locusts, leeches, plague, foxes, snakes, insects, lice.* With the first installment of his Viennese salary, her husband once took her to the Burgtheater. They sat in the cheapest seats and saw *Iphigenia on Tauris.* "Farewell," she remembers. At the time, she imagined she understood better than anyone else in the theater, at that final moment before the curtain closed, what it meant to renounce something. Never did she see her mother reading the *Collected Works* of Goethe, but now, every one of its volumes is standing there in her grandmother's bookshelf, tidily arranged next to the miniature grandfather clock, just the same as back home. So that's why the suitcase her mother brought with her to Vienna was so heavy. Farewell. All her life she's paid for having snatched her first child back from hell with nothing more than a handful of snow, and only now is it becoming clear that there are things that have no price. *No breath of air disturbs the place. / Deathly silence far and wide. / O'er the ghastly deeps no single / Wavelet ripples with the tide.* Was she the one her mother had brought these books to? She also packs the seven-armed candelabra from the sideboard in the suitcase. *Zay moykhl un fal mir mayne trep nit arunter.* Don't go falling down the stairs. Now it is too late to speak Yiddish with her mother. A number of the windows facing the courtyard in the stairwell have been replaced with wooden panels. She can't see the angel above the entryway because she doesn't turn around. She would like to know what exactly her mother had been paying for all her life. At home, in Volume 9, the spine of which is a bit scraped, she finds the play that for the most part she can still recite by heart. She doesn't make a fire in the stove, she doesn't wash the dishes, she doesn't go stand in line, she doesn't sew, doesn't darn and doesn't cry; she sits down quietly in the kitchen, wrapped in blankets, and just as she did back when she was a young girl, she reads Goethe's play *Iphigenia*.

31

The father doesn't die until just over a year later, on December 2, 1920. His wife sells his clothes on the black market, but first she cuts off the gold-colored buttons with the eagle of the monarchy and puts them in a box. The father's December salary, paid out to the widow as a final installment, is just enough for one midday meal. At least the daughter gets an extra portion of milk with cocoa each day at school, thanks to the Americans.

32

In 1944 in a small forest of birch trees, a notebook filled with handwritten diary entries will fall to the ground when a sentry uses his rifle butt to push a young woman forward, and she tries to protect herself with arms she had previously been using to clutch the notebook to her chest. The book will fall in the mud, and the woman will not be able to return to pick it up again. For a while the book will remain lying there, wind and rain will turn its pages, footsteps will pass over it, until all the secrets written there are the same color as the mud.

INTERMEZZO

But if her grandmother had left for the Vienna Woods just half an hour later to gather firewood; or if the young woman who was so eager to cast her life aside had not, after leaving her grandmother's locked door to wander through the city, taken a right turn from Babenberger Strasse onto Opernring, where she coincidentally encountered her own death in the form of a shabby young man; or if the fiancée of this shabby young man had not broken off their engagement until the next day; or if the shabby young man's father hadn't left his Mauser pistol in the unlocked drawer of his desk; if the young woman hadn't looked from behind like a girl of easy virtue because her skirt was just too short—why in the world had she cut it half a year before; or, given how cold it was, if she'd crossed Babenberger Strasse in the icy spot despite the danger of slipping (instead of protecting herself from this danger with healthy instincts only to run right into the arms of death moments later with all her limbs intact), indeed, if she had slipped and fallen, perhaps even broken a leg, then she would have been brought to the Vienna General Hospital to have her leg set in plaster, instead of several days later, in the bloom of health, succumbing to a violent death of her own choosing and winding up in a chilly storage room; or if the frigid weather sweeping in from Sweden had given way to the warm Gulf stream two days earlier, then her grandmother wouldn't have needed to go to the Vienna Woods until that Wednesday, or the puddle wouldn't have been frozen, and when the young woman came to the end of Babenberger Strasse, she would certainly have made the decision to cross the street at that point and walk past the Vienna Museum of Fine Arts, which would have been closed that Sunday evening—she'd once seen a picture there of a family consisting of a father, grandmother, and child—and at that moment, she would have been thinking not about having herself shot, but about the lemon the father was holding out to the child, that brightly glowing bit of yellow in the dark painting that, during these hours when the museum was closed, was now hanging on a wall unseen. Who decides what thoughts time will be filled with? Only half an hour, or perhaps an entire hour later, becoming conscious that her only option for a bed that night was at her parents' apartment, she would have turned around, would have walked down the Ring, but this time in the direction of home, since she wouldn't have had the money for a taxi, and while her homeward journey would still have taken her past the opera house, the young man would have no longer been waiting there on Opernring, he would long since have been lying—for the price of two pounds of butter, fifty decagrams of veal, and ten candles—in the arms of some girl of easy virtue, while she herself would have gone home unmolested, would to be sure have been obliged to ring the concierge's bell, waking her, and then to ask her mother to pay the twenty-heller fee, for which her mother would have reproached her, but these reproaches would only have strengthened her resolve to start earning her own money as soon as possible so as to finally be able to move out of her parents' apartment and rent a room of her own. But the decisive moment was probably not the one that had just passed, it was everything that had come before. There was an entire world of reasons why her life had now reached its end, just as there was an entire world of reasons why she could and should remain alive.

★

The decision to move out of her parents' apartment is one she would have made that evening in any case, whether it was sitting with a broken leg in the waiting room of the General Hospital, in the Vienna Woods with her grandmother's rucksack strapped to her back, or on her grandmother's sofa, shivering beneath a thin blanket after her grandmother offered to let her spend the night. *If you can't go up, you'll have to go down—but if you can't go across, you still have to go across.* Most probably, though, she'd have been lying at home in her own bed, and in the other bed would be her sleeping sister: this little sister who was already five foot seven; and if she'd been certain that her sister's slumber, though restless, was nonetheless sound, she would have gotten up again to retrieve her diary from its hiding place behind the wardrobe and with a small pencil—writing in the dark, blind—she would have written an entry about everything that had happened. Just as at the age of fourteen, in the midst of hunger, she had resolved not to let hunger blackmail her any longer, she would now have resolved, in the midst of her unhappy love, not to let herself be blackmailed by unhappy love. If she had managed to avoid the one place in Vienna and the one moment of the evening that could have translated her desire to cast her life away into a death, she would now have realized, while writing in her diary, that in fact writing was the only thing she wanted to do to make money, and she would have started to consider how and what she could write, and so for the first time in this entire week of misery she would have been thinking about something other than the man she loved and her own shame and unhappiness.

The next morning she would have no longer have been able to decipher what she'd written, since in the darkness of the night before, she'd have inscribed half and whole letters one on top of the other in a single line. The shabby young man would have remained

115

hale and unscathed, and a few years later, at twenty-five, he would already have developed a bald spot. Her grandmother would not have fallen down the cellar stairs, and more than a decade later she would have hidden her granddaughter for several days when she was threatened with arrest; but under these circumstances, her father would not have postponed his own death and would have died on March 2 of this same year, just five weeks after this night, of heart failure. Standing beside his grave, his older daughter would involuntarily have thought for a second time of the lemon the Gothic father held out to his child—whether it was a boy or girl was uncertain—in the midst of all that darkness. She would have taken possession of her father's excerpts from *Notes on Earthquakes in Styria* and, weeping as she wrote, used them for her very first article: "May the earth gape open once more and swallow up the war profiteers!" For although her father died in his bed—of myocardial insufficiency, the doctors said—she was convinced that in the end he had died of the war.

Her mother would have been paid the March installment of her husband's salary, which at that moment was just enough for the current week's groceries.

BOOK III

1

A woman sits at a desk writing an account of her life. The desk is in Moscow. This is the third time in her life she's been asked to write an account of it, and it's entirely possible that this written account will put an end to her life, possible that this piece of writing will be transformed, if you will, into a weapon to be used against her. It's also possible that this piece of writing will be kept in reserve and that from the moment she turns it in she'll be obliged to live up to it, or to prove herself worthy of it, or else confirm the darkest suspicions that might arise from it. In the last case, the words she's writing here would also—after a brief or protracted delay—be something like a misdiagnosed illness that eventually, inevitably, would kill her. Didn't her husband always say that in the theater there's never a gun hanging on the wall that isn't going to be fired off at some point? She remembers Ibsen's *The Wild Duck* and how she wept when the shot was finally fired. But perhaps she'll succeed—after all that's why she's sitting here, her one hope, and the reason she is taking such pains to find just the right words—perhaps she'll succeed in writing herself a way out, in extending her life by means of a few letters more or less, or at least making her life less onerous; there's nothing left for her to hope for now than to succeed in using her writing to write her way back into life. But what are the right words? Would a truth take her farther than a lie? And which of the many possible truths or lies should she use? When she doesn't even know who will be reading what she writes?

There's only one thing she doesn't assume: that this piece of writing will be nothing more than a sheet of paper with ink on it, slipped into a folder and forgotten. In a country in which every child and every cleaning woman and every soldier can recite poems by Lermontov and Pushkin from memory, that would not be likely.

2

I was born in 1902 in Brody to a civil servant and his wife, in other words I had a bourgeois background. And what exactly made this background bourgeois? Perhaps the fact that when her grandmother fled from Galicia to Vienna more than twenty years ago, she dragged along an edition of Goethe's *Collected Works*? Her father's salary wasn't enough for her parents to employ a maid even during their very first years in Vienna. She never had piano lessons, nor did her sister play the violin. She knows of course that her background is considered bourgeois because her father, instead of being a factory worker, was an official at the Meteorological Institution. *I earn my money with my buttocks,* he liked to say, meaning all the hours he spent in a chair poring over data. Even so they'd nearly starved. Despite this fact, both her first account of her life, which she'd written when she applied for a visa to enter the Soviet Union, and the second one, composed apropos of her unsuccessful bid to be admitted into the Soviet Union's Communist Party, were marred by this bourgeois background of hers, as no doubt this third one would be as well. Her background stuck to her, there was no helping it, and she was stuck to it as well. She'd been able to remake her thinking from scratch, but not her family history.

Never would she possess the same level of freedom as her husband, who was free for all time, *doubly free*—and in principle free even now that he was in prison, since he'd completed an apprenticeship as a metalworker before beginning to write, he'd been a laborer, a *doubly free laborer*; in other words: possessing nothing that could tie him down, he could go anywhere he wanted. From a societal perspective, he was immune to blackmail. *The working class has nothing to lose but their chains.* But did she herself really have more to lose? Had she perhaps inherited not only the myopia but also the fearfulness of her father, who all his life was obliged to worry that some trifling offense might prevent him from rising on schedule from one pay grade to the next and in the worst-case scenario—a revolution, say—even cause him to lose his position? Were hands by nature more honest than heads? As a young girl, how she would have loved to work with her hands, creating something that hadn't previously existed—but ever since that day at school when a crafts teacher had held up the doll's dress she had made, presenting it for the entire class to see as an example of what she called *shoddy* and *sloppy* work, since this day at school she had lost her faith in the work of her hands. If there were such a thing as being born to grace, there was probably also a gracelessness you could be born to. *Sloppy* and *shoddy*. She had later made the workers' struggle her own all the more fervently.

In 1909 my family relocated to Vienna. Prolonged adversity spurred me to become politically active for the first time at age fourteen, spearheading an anti-war demonstration in 1916. Since I had not yet benefited from Marxist schooling, it was merely an outpouring of pacifist sentiment that prompted my resistance.

In her first account of her life, written as part of her visa application, she had gone on at this point, writing: . . . *but my resistance arose out of a passionate hatred of the war. Was the birth of the Soviet Union in 1917 not also identical with the decision on the part of the Bolsheviks, alone among all the peoples of the world, to autonomously cast off the burden of this inhuman war, despite the enormous sacrifices this required?*

If the world revolution had succeeded in those days, the uniting of the proletarians of all countries would have been not only the start of a new world but also of an eternal peace. What cause could people possibly have to slaughter one another? What cause could the Austrians have to make the Italians bleed, what cause the Germans to slit open the French? None at all.

To be sure, there had been peace in 1918, but the European borders were not dissolved, they were only pushed this way and that. On the other hand, everything outside the Soviet Union, the border between those who worked and those who lived off others' labor, remained right where it was. Ever since the start of this miserable peace nearly twenty years ago, the young Soviet power stood all on its own against a united front of European reactionaries—in a new war, the Soviets would be not one enemy among others, but the sole enemy. And this war would surely not be long in coming. From where she sat today, she cast a critical glance at the young peace-loving girl she once had been. She had understood even then that there was a difference between the blood that flowed during a revolution and the blood that was spilled in a war. She also knew that all wars are not created equal.

After the end of the war and my father's death, still working in complete political isolation, I began to write antimilitaristic articles that I submitted to the Workers' Journal—*unsuccessfully at the time—while also writing my first novel,* Sisyphus.

She wasn't just politically isolated back then—she was completely alone. And lonely. But she doesn't write that. Still, something that at the time was nearly her undoing proved to be a blessing in disguise: recently she heard that the man she'd once almost killed herself over was a longstanding member of a Trotskyist group. He'd been known as W. back when she first met him, then she encountered him again as Comrade E. at an assembly, and later—like so many of them, herself included—he had meandered through various identities, becoming Za., whose articles she sometimes read, later going by P. when he was in hiding, as a comrade once told her, but she hadn't known what name he'd been using recently for his work in Leningrad. Over the past few months she'd occasionally heard mention of the Trotskyist, Zinovievist, and Bukharinist Lü., but it never occurred to her to suspect this was the same man she'd once been so in love with. Only a few weeks ago, when she happened to see a photograph of a defendant named Lü. in the newspaper, she had recognized him.

I demand . . .
During the Spanish Civil War . . .
An unacceptable . . .
Where I was, not at a congress.
I must object most vigorously.
In the trenches . . .
Could also have taken a different path.
When F. tried to pin the blame on me . . .
And since then never again. I demand . . .
Delayed detonation, surely you can . . .
Why all this beating around the bush?
Lü., his closest friend . . .
With me? Never!
This beating around the bush . . .
Br., just one . . .
F. is sowing suspicions . . .
Cannot work like this . . .
Not in the hinterlands!
A functionary who writes on the side, not an author.
A clear path.
I ask myself why Br. is not presenting an argument.
And I ask myself why F. is unleashing his cynical . . .
Taken into consideration as well.

Why is F. so intensely pessimistic?

Have any of you . . . how two-faced?

Neither a productive nor a constructive . . .

Br.'s sectarianism to closer scrutiny.

Rather, on the contrary, quite harmful.

Just look at the introduction and the sentences altered in the Russian version.

That isn't true.

The introduction is . . .

That isn't true!

Not forward-thinking.

Empty allegations and underhanded . . .

The introduction is not the same.

Do you mean to claim . . .

I'm not alleging anything, I'd just like . . . it's not the same as in the Russian version.

Do you mean to claim that . . .

Nothing more to say on the subject.

Declare my resignation.

I too lay down my post.

Why don't we just go ahead and dissolve . . .

Perhaps we should . . .

I really have nothing more to say on the subject.

We might in fact in the presence of . . .

A reprimand might be . . .

But not in the presence of . . .

Why in the world?

Of a Party representative.

Leave me out of it.

During this period I supported myself by working at a stationery shop. In none of these accounts has she written that she often used to nap during her lunch hour on the paper-filled shelves in the back room of this small shop. The cousin who owned the shop had given her permission. The large sheets of paper were fresher than any bed-sheet, and just as if she were getting into bed, she always took off her shoes before she filed herself away in one of these compartments. She was constantly tired during those first few months when she was no longer living with her mother and sister, constantly tired because she was spending her nights writing her novel. She had so often wished for her father to return to life, and perhaps she succeeded, perhaps her words did bring him back to life again, assuming they were the right words.

Several times a quiet young man had purchased red paper from her, then asked her to cut it to leaflet size right there in the shop with the big cutting machine. Silently, he had watched her set up the machine and then turn the big crank to slice through an entire stack of paper at one go. *I first made contact with the Communist Party of Austria through Comrade G.* At some point she had spotted a wayward handbill, now printed, lying in the gutter, and had recognized its color. She picked up the leaflet and began to read.

Comrade G. didn't come into the shop again all summer, but when he appeared in September, he looked at her not with two open eyes but only one and a half. He now resembled the enormous weary lizard that had been put on display in the Schönbrunn Menagerie, one of the few post-war acquisitions.

While he was standing beside her at the cutting machine, watching her arrange the stack of paper, she asked:

An accident?

Someone knocked me down and beat me.

Really?

A soldier.

A soldier?

Yes.

Why?

The putsch.

She'd read about it. On Hörligasse, a handful of Communists had even been killed, but here in the Alser District, life had gone on as before.

And your eye?

It won't stop watering.

I'm sorry.

While she was cranking the wheel that pressed the stack of paper together, it occurred to her that from now on it would never again be possible to tell for sure whether this quiet man perhaps had reason to weep, or whether it was just his eye shedding tears on its own.

Would you like to come some time?

While she was slicing through the stack of paper at one go, he wiped his damp cheek with the back of his hand and told her that his Communist cell always met on Wednesdays.

I see.

So it was possible to sacrifice your health and possibly even your life for something other than love, you could keep yourself preserved until it was time to throw your life and body into the jaws of time for a good cause.

But in Hungary it's all over already, she said, meaning the Hungarian Soviet Republic.

We're learning, he said, and the world still has no idea what is happening here, but soon it will be astonished.

It would also never again be possible to tell for sure whether he was laughing so hard there were tears rolling down his cheeks or just laughing, she thought, and she began to wrap the freshly sliced stack of paper in paper.

The comrade who is me and Comrade B. are walking down Tverskaya when the comrade who is me sees him. He is walking on the other side of the street. He waves to the comrade who is me. The comrade who is me waves as well, and I ask, Shouldn't we call him over to our side of the street? For God's sake, what if someone sees us! If someone sees us, he'll see he was only waving to the comrade who is me. I beckon, and he comes over, B. turns away. We stroll up and down Strastnoy several times. The conversation is superficial. We discuss lighting, the use of a greenish light. His tone is cordial. We spend approximately a quarter hour together. Then he says goodbye. Should it now be considered an error that the comrade who is me and Comrade B. spoke to him? In any case, we spoke to him.

One Wednesday, for the first time in her life, she met people who didn't just grumble about how awful everything was, but instead clearheadedly investigated why this machine known as progress kept undermining the well-being of mankind.

Otherwise, what was the point of being young in a time like this when progress itself was still young, one of them asked—a man the others called Comrade H.—and with a quick toss of his head, he flipped a strand of hair off his forehead, a gesture she would later come to know so well.

It is not enough to be eighteen years old.

Now that mankind had finally, thanks to the inventions of the modern age, acquired the means to raise itself above the limitations imposed by the need for survival, it was now time for them to ensure that mankind was actually taking advantage of these means, cried a pudgy comrade known as A. and he got to his feet to describe the rising up of humanity with a powerful sweep of his arm. And not, he went on, so as to pile up immeasurable wealth for just a few individuals, not so as to conquer new markets and cheaper sites of production through the subjugation of the colonies, to simply redistribute natural resources in the next war. No! We are standing at a beginning, he exclaimed, not somewhere in the middle, but right at the starting point—and again he scooped up a mighty armful of air and shoved this air across to the middle of the table, dispersing the cloud of smoke that had gathered there and sending it swirling in all directions. Then he sat down again to roll himself a fresh cigarette.

It is not enough to be eighteen years old.

Comrade U., who spoke quietly so that people would listen to her, said, nearly whispering, that the distribution of the generated revenues would have to be regulated, since the moment it was possible for an individual to enrich himself, that's what he'd do.

Precisely, H. said, adding that it was in any case high time to take private ownership to the cleaners, time for mankind to become one with itself, on a truly massive scale! Those who have never been allowed to use their teeth for anything more than biting their tongues should now be fed and allowed to digest and grow—even to take a crap! he shouted, laughing as he bared his own teeth. Flesh to flesh, he cried, flipping back his strand of hair.

Beautiful Z. smiled, and Comrade U., once more speaking at the edge of audibility, opined that Comrade H. was perhaps going a bit too far, but that in principle he was probably not wrong: the massively widespread alienation of labor could only be a preliminary phase that would eventually lead to a world in which the masses would also benefit from these massive quantities of labor.

Well, that's no laughing matter, G. said, and his eye started watering again, making it impossible to tell whether he was laughing so hard there were tears rolling down his cheeks or perhaps crying, or neither of the two; no laughing matter, he said, and besides: If we can tame Nature, which completely surrounds us, surely we can prevent human selfishness from casting us back into an animal state.

No, youth no longer existed so one could squander one's youth, or simply wait for the years to pass until one could eventually slip into old age as into rags that others had worn to shreds. It no longer existed for being ground down to make up for the failings of an older generation. Now the point of youth was to be thrown away: for a new world such as the world had never seen before.

They were all in a good mood, they were singing and drinking coffee.

When I was there, all they were doing was dancing. I can't dance, it was a dull two hours for me.

We showed up and played cards. We didn't have any particular conversations.

They were already having coffee. There was no discussion of politics at all.

V. sometimes turned up at my apartment, which I took to mean that he liked to smoke and drink for free. I saw no political motivation for his behavior.

And so V. was in my room on several occasions, mainly we talked about bygone days. In early November 1935 I had one last brief encounter with him on the street.

After the fall of 1931 I never saw him again. We weren't at all close, neither personally nor politically.

Once he came and sat with me as I was drinking a glass of beer. He made a very bad impression on me. I never saw him again.

He can't hold his drink at all. Usually the first glass is enough for him.

Sometimes he's just pretending!

That's right, I've seen that.

Did Comrade Br. ever run into Comrade T. at V.'s apartment?

Not that I recall, but it's always possible. I'd rather err on the side of assuming he did.

Why do you consider this a possibility?

According to what I've heard, the two of them knew each other.

S., L., M., and O. were once there too. A female journalist from Sweden was there, then K. and Sch. Once H. with his wife, and besides them, Comrade R., and Ö. with his wife—I think that's all of them.

I was there once, too.

Oh, right, Fr. and also C.

Pretty much everyone was tipsy.

I consider it my duty to emphatically put a stop to these evenings, no matter how festive. When alcohol is being consumed, it is impossible to monitor whether a political remark is being made that can no longer be monitored.

I was at his apartment once on New Year's Eve when the entire place was
   full and there were a large number of comrades in attendance.
Was I there?
No.
Was I there?
No.
Me?
No.
Once I went to his apartment because he had invited me ten times.
I was off traveling all the time, so I didn't have any sort of relationship
   with V. at all.
That V. managed to escape being unmasked by us as two-faced until the
   very end is of course quite disconcerting. The moral I draw from this is
   that his behavior was not entirely correct.

One evening after a meeting, she had told H. about her *Sisyphus*,
and he had talked to her about his plays. A few days later the two
of them went together to a gathering of so-called revolutionary
writers, and suddenly everything that had been separate for so long
and separately had made no sense fell into place. After all what did
having a world view mean if not learning to see? Was it possible to
change the world if you found the right words? Could the world
be changed only if you happened to find them?

The question of whether Comrade O., who had written something about the murder of Rosa Luxemburg, was permitted to describe the *Freikorps* soldier as meticulously as she did his victim was
really about whether she was allowed to know in advance what
she was writing or whether, on the contrary, it was her duty to be
constantly searching. It was also a question about the irreversibil-
ity of good and evil, in short, fundamentally, about whether people could be educated, about whether hope had boundaries or not.
Whether this or that classic author, while writing, was a participant
in his time or whether he stood outside it as an observer was as

much a question of life and death as the question of whom the factories belonged to. Was a revolutionary poem in sonnet form a capitulation to the enemy, a retreat in disguise, and was poet J.—cat hair on his sweater, his teeth brown from smoking—perhaps trying to imprison the revolution in fourteen lines? Everything would have been different if the social-democratic pigs hadn't locked up our leadership back in June. Sitting in this gathering, she had felt for the first time in her life that literature itself was something real, just as real as a bag of flour, a pair of shoes, or a crowd being stirred to revolt. Here the words themselves were something you could touch, there was no transition from literature to what was called reality—instead, the sentences themselves were a reality. Van Gogh had cut off his own ear, why shouldn't it hurt just as much when a figure in a play cut off someone else in the middle of a speech? Was it in order to write that the Communists had come into this world? Did every word matter?

Unfortunately I was often not present at these gatherings, because I was one of the ones who didn't get invited. My temperament is fairly volatile at times, and Comrade F. took such offense at my outbursts that he called me a worm. If I were to sink to that level, I might say he was a hopeless drunk. I won't say that, because I don't want to sink to his level. Of course I make mistakes. I would like to practice ruthless self-criticism. I am insanely despised by Comrade M. and also by Comrade C., whose garrulousness is quite distressing to me, by the way. Now I'm having to prove that I am clean; M. doesn't have to prove that he is right. It upsets me when Comrade M. forgets my name when he's reading out the list of contributors. What an expression of disrespect. Of course, I don't mean to say I think he's engaging in this sort of politicking as an agent of fascism. I repeat that I cannot prove anything. I had an argument with Comrade C. I began to commit errors. Suddenly, I was taking offense at personal styles of communication, which I never would have done before. Gossip here, gossip there, and then there was the matter at hand. If I remember correctly, it seemed as if C. was constantly pregnant with miscarriages. I insist that by saying these things I am not revealing anything. I'm fighting to have someone finally tell me in a straightforward manner what is going on. What sorts of allegations do you have against me? I am fighting for my honor. I demand that Comrade M. stand up and explain why I wasn't invited to contribute. Let Comrade M. stand up and let Comrade C. be called in as well. I know my own errors perfectly well. But I don't want to hear the excuse that I didn't turn in my articles on time. I met V. here in Moscow and could smell right away that he stank, like a dog that's always pushing its way into things and can't look you in the eye. Besides, he told lies. I immediately reported this to the cadre leadership. Every comrade has flaws, if a person says he has no flaws, this means he hasn't done any self-criticism. By the way: V. always regarded me with the greatest contempt and condescension, which is something I cannot abide, especially when there's no call for it. In my view, it ought to be possible to eliminate a fellow like that from the territory of the Soviet Union. What is going on? If I speak openly now, from comrade to comrade, I might wind up making a remark that will break my neck. Wouldn't it be better for us to help one another? I came to Moscow, and a tall fellow with curly hair came to see me. An individual too dim-witted to engage in any sort of work but who is easy prey for any counterrevolutionary element. He brought me a few poems. They were so unbelievably bad that I felt sick to my stomach. I don't ask to be given a medal of honor, all I ask is that if I am going to be politically isolated, a political explanation be given. I'm not the only one who comes into this room and can't shake the feeling that a couple of the people here are keeping secrets from a third individual, or a fourth, a fifth, or sixth. The cell must demand absolute openness. At the moment there is only a single person not trying to play me for a sucker, and that is me.

One evening it was her turn to read a few pages aloud from her *Sisyphus* manuscript for the first time. Sch., the man in the yellow suit jacket—her name for him to this day—voiced the criticism that the book centered around a petit-bourgeois main character. Was it not precisely this petit-bourgeois indecisiveness that had caused the June Uprising to fail? Did she mean to identify with it? What about progress? But Comrade O, the only older woman in this circle, replied in her hoarse voice that it was progress when one paid heed to the truth, as this young author was most certainly doing. Before striding off upon a new path, must one not have acquired a profound understanding of what was wrong with the old one? Sallow, mustached K. replied with a certain acerbity: Of course you can invest a great deal of effort into always trying to understand everything, but we would still be tugging away at the Gordian Knot if it hadn't occurred to someone to just slice through it. J., a poet—cat hair on his sweater, his teeth brown from smoking—said that he particularly liked the leisurely pace of her storytelling, and the many repetitions, because they reflected the stagnation from which the book's hero suffered. Exactly, H. said: for once a story was being told via the language as well and not just the plot—and if they, the revolutionary authors, really were hoping to create a new Adam, the only clay they had at their disposal was language! His strand of hair fell in his face, but he didn't notice. Hereupon Comrade T., raising her voice more than was necessary to be heard in this small gathering, declared that when an author resorted to gimmicks to make the reader pay attention to the writing, the text lost all power to point to something beyond itself, and she found that a shame. Not a shame, sallow, mustached K. added, but possibly dangerous, because a person who is enjoying something stays right where he is and stops moving forward. Had she been writing at the brink of an abyss, and just in time found friends who could drag her back from its edge? Had her text, which she had written in isolation, now been transformed into something that—through all these critiques and expressions of support—would bind her to these friends more intimately than a kiss might among young people who were merely eighteen years old? She was hurt by what Comrade T. said, while H.'s words, spoken this time without

133

flipping the hair out of his face, sent happiness coursing dizzily through her body down to her fingertips, but neither Comrade T. nor H. was indifferent to what she thought and wondered. Indifference did not exist within this circle; here, every word mattered. *It is not enough to be eighteen years old.*

By joining the Communist Party, she had catapulted herself into the middle of this life. She, too, was now one of those in whose bodies and souls the present had finally found itself after centuries of inertia and was beginning to race forward; it was a present far too large and swift for one person alone, but together they would be able to hold their ground upon the crest of time, even when it was traveling at a gallop. In her account of her life, all of this is represented by a single sentence: *In 1920 I joined the Communist Party of Austria; I was vouched for by Comrade G., the intellectual pioneer of the Communist movement, and Comrade U., who at the time ran the local group Vienna-Margareten.*

She is required to list those who vouched for her, even though U.— who has since been expelled from the Party and condemned to death in absentia for high treason by the Soviet courts—now lives in Paris. In other words, she was vouched for by a leftist sectarian back when she was young. Did they mean to pin her down as the young person she had been, her very youth now a cause for reproach?

In her first account of her life, the name U. had still been worth dropping. *Comrade U., now a respected functionary of the Communist International, and Comrade G., the intellectual pioneer of the Communist movement, vouched for me when I joined the Communist Party of Austria in 1920.*

In the second account, written when she was applying to be accepted into the Communist Party of the Soviet Union, she had simply said: *Comrade G., the intellectual pioneer of the Communist movement, and Comrade U. vouched for me.*

By that time, the *respected functionary of the Communist International* was no longer taking part in Comintern assemblies and held no position of any sort; a rumor was circulating that she had conspired with Kirov's murderers, but no one knew exactly how.

Now, in this third account of her life, she explains: *At the time I was influenced by U., an enemy of the people, and while I was not an active participant in the debates being held at the time, I did, like her, take an approving stance in our group's discussions of the meaning of the June Uprising of 1919, thereby unintentionally contributing to the formation of factions which caused damage to the Austrian Communist Party.*

And so the past moved through the movements taking place in the present. But could looking at things in a certain way really change the things themselves?

When her father died shortly after the end of the war, she was convinced that he had died of the war, even though he'd been nowhere near the front: what had killed him was profound exhaustion after years of struggling to support a family under catastrophic circumstances.

Her mother, on the other hand, had shouted after her down the stairs when she was moving out of her parents' apartment the spring after her father's death that her father obviously hadn't been able to stomach seeing his older daughter doing everything in her power to go to the dogs.

Her little sister, to be sure, did not share her mother's opinion that the older girl was to blame for their father's death, but she was just as disinclined to agree with her sister that their father had privately capitulated. It was out of protest against the modern age, she told her older sister, an insurrection of his heart against life's unreasonable demands—in other words, it was basically his strength and radicalism that drove him to his death, and these are both things you inherited, she said.

The older girl replied that she was unfortunately unable to believe that retreating could count as a protest.

But it does, the younger one said, it really does! Only through his death, she said, did their father finally succeed in returning to where he'd basically wanted to be ever since 1917: at the side of the late Kaiser, and in his own way he had declared the modern age bankrupt.

Unfortunately, the modern age doesn't give a damn about his opinion, the older girl said.

Death can also be a sort of strike!

Hmm, the big sister said, I don't know.

But then the two girls had already reached the entrance to the building, and the older one didn't want to go upstairs for fear of running into their mother.

And so each of them—she herself, her mother, and her sister, too—described her father's death in quite different terms, even though the fact of his death confronted all of them in equal measure; each of them assigned it a different cause and meaning, as though it could be spoken of only in terms of this or that story, as a sort of dead stub that in some form or other had fused with each of their lives. Each called his death by another name, and probably this naming helped them to at least obscure the fact hidden behind the name, if not forget it outright, to prevent this gaping maw from possibly luring those who remained alive down into the underworld.

The doctors, though, following the dictates of their profession, recorded with the utmost objectivity nothing more than the scientific explanation for her father's end in the Registry of Deaths: *myocardial insufficiency*.

She couldn't help thinking of this the first time she read the Manifesto of the Communist Party, when she began to hope that perhaps there was a doctor who could treat the severe illnesses from which mankind as a whole was suffering.

*

As she heads to the common kitchen to fetch some hot water from the samovar for her tea, a wind rises up far away on a bit of steppe, 45.61404 degrees latitude north, 70.75195 degrees longitude east, collecting a few grains of sand that get caught amid the blades of grass, while other grains of sand lying beside the tufts are carried off. For weeks now it hasn't rained there. A beetle, emerging from nowhere, on its way nowhere, passes the time by creeping up one of the grass blades, where, having reached the top, it turns around again and goes on its way facing down. The blade of grass bent a little beneath the weight of the beetle when it reached the tip— bent almost imperceptibly, since the beetle's weight was so slight, but still it was something. Now that the six-legged visitor has returned to earth and is once more making its laborious way among the other stalks belonging to this tuft of grass, the stalk is standing erect again, trembling ever so slightly from time to time in the tranquil air we describe as a lull.

The Jews, she thinks on her way back to her room, knew what they were doing when they decided never to call God by his name. Lenin once wrote that a glass was not only indisputably a cylinder made of glass, it was also a drinking vessel; it was not just a heavy object such as might be used for throwing, but could also serve as a paper-weight, or to hold a trapped butterfly. Lenin had read Hegel, and Hegel in turn had said that truth was the whole. She always used to drink tea with her husband late into the night. Now she is sitting here alone. Could it be a mistake to have Lenin's *Philosophical Notebooks* right there on her shelf? Has Lenin been outlawed yet? Could he have been a classic author when she set out to get her tea, but already a criminal by the time she returns with her cup? He lies across the Neva from her in his coffin made of glass; if he were to turn over, everyone would see.

This was a weekend in early spring, perhaps around Easter. A lake outside Berlin.

Utterly disgraceful, someone should put a stop to it, such a ne'er-do-well.

We wanted to paddle across in our kayak.

Serves him right.

I remember that the weather was not on our side that day.

Turned out to lack all talent.

It seemed as if winter was moving in on us again.

We did ask ourselves what detours had brought him here and wondered about the strange writer's life he was leading. Then we said: Why get involved with filth like that?

It snowed that last night, there was even sleet. Thin sheets of ice were floating around on the lake, but they broke apart as soon as the prow of our boat touched them.

A handful of comrades thought he had a gift.

That evening he read us his latest story in parting.

Gifted—that can mean all sorts of things.

The next day we went our separate ways.

We cannot continue to employ the designation "gifted" if he is being expelled from the organization as a writer of trash.

Hurriedly, and in fine spirits, our friend strolled off. One week later he left for Moscow.

Only a single person said he agreed with me, in a whisper: it was him. Dear comrade, I said, if you share this opinion, do stand up and say so aloud. He said that he would, but soon after he disappeared.

He stopped just the one time, to turn around and wave to us.

Shocking what he tried to pull.

I shall always see his face before me.

Tried to incite me to . . .

His solid, almost stocky figure.

To say that the book is garbage . . .

His closely shorn, stubbly hair.

Unmasked in his dream of being a writer, just in time.

Those watchful eyes . . .
Banished from literature.
. . . that were now filled with joyful expectation.
The case involving the existence of a group in Moscow with an absolute
idiot at its head—the individual in question—has now been rectified.

3

A good friend of her husband's, the theater director N., had given her and her husband a letter of introduction to Yagoda, the head of the secret service, when they emigrated to the Soviet Union. Her husband didn't want to use it, why not, she said, he said: cronyism isn't Socialism, and he flipped the strand of hair out of his face, she said, that isn't cronyism, it's just one comrade lending another a helping hand. If we do our work well, we won't need any help, her husband said, then he tore up the letter and threw it in the wastepaper basket. Meanwhile Yagoda has been relieved of his duties, arrested, and—recently, during the third show trial—indicted, then condemned to death and executed. Perhaps Yagoda's successors are coming up the stairs this very moment. Did her husband really tear up the letter of introduction, or did she—as she sometimes imagined, dreamed, or perhaps even really remembered during the nights following his arrest—retrieve the scraps of paper from the wastebasket, glue them together, and put the document back in the drawer? Then it would be found now and would provide a justification for her arrest. She absolutely must finish the account of her life before she is arrested. Then this piece of writing can do battle with that letter, assuming someone really has found it, or will find it and wish to use it as evidence against her and her husband: paper against paper.

With the roller to the side of her typewriter, she scrolls back up the last eight lines, then strikes the "X" key over and over until the paragraph she has just written becomes illegible. Then she goes on writing.

Active in.
While fighting.
Journey to.
At work on.
He, he, and she.

Hitler's victory in the election most certainly spelled defeat for the German working classes, but at the time could one really describe it as a defeat for the Communist Party of Germany, as her husband had done?

Sch., the man in the yellow suit jacket—now a delegate to the Communist International—had replied to her husband: If the Social Democrats hadn't drawn a line between themselves and the Communists, but instead had joined with the Communists to create a united front against the Nazis, there wouldn't have been a majority for Hitler.

We didn't lose the workers to social democracy, we lost them to the Fascists, her husband had said, and then asked: Why? Because of this question—which he had ultimately been asking himself, not the delegate to the Communist International—he had been severely chastised by the Party, and demoted to performing lower-level Party work.

Her husband had spent one year in Berlin without papers collecting membership dues from a group of five Party members.

Shortly after her husband had left for Germany, she went for a walk on frozen Lake Neusiedl with her friend G. and asked him whether they ought to wish that Marx had been wrong, in other words that when capitalism went to seed, it wasn't because the petit bourgeois had slid down into the proletariat, but because the proletariat had slid upwards into the petite bourgeoisie and in their new capacity as petit bourgeois had voted for Hitler.

But what about the working classes?

Marx was not mistaken, her friend G. said. The working classes had voted for Hitler, but H. was still wrong in his theory that the Communist Party had been defeated.

But Hitler is leading the workers into the next war to defend the interests of Big Capital, leading them to the slaughter! Haven't people always said: A vote for Hitler is a vote for war?

The worse this war turns out to be, G. said, the better for us. For the masses to turn away from him and come running into our arms, we need the crimes he is about to commit to be as huge as possible.

She looked down to contemplate this sentence, looked at the thin layer of snow lying upon the ice, and thought about how shallow the water in this lake was. The lake was enormous, but when you swam in it during the summer, there was no point where the water reached higher than your neck.

She didn't see her husband again until 1934, in Prague, and from there the two of them applied for a visa to the Soviet Union. Shortly after their arrival in Moscow, they heard Dimitrov speak at the Seventh World Congress of the Communist International. In his speech he said the same thing as her husband two years before: If the Social Democrats hadn't drawn a line between themselves and the Communists, but instead had joined with the Communists to create a united front against the Nazis, there wouldn't have been a majority for Hitler.

But what was right could only be right when it was uttered and codified by the Party, that's what the Party was there for: to be the wisdom of many, not the wisdom of one. An individual might lose his head, but not an entire Party.

Instead of taking on Hitler jointly, Communists and Social Democrats jointly erred; on the basis of two carefully differentiated, but equally faulty, assessments of the situation, they apparently arrived at two carefully differentiated but equally faulty positions. The Social Democrats described the Communists as *radicalinskis*, as terrorists and subversives, while the Communists decried the Social Democrats as the murderers of the workers, the slaves of Big Capital and *Social Fascists*. Once labels of this sort were applied, an alliance was no longer possible. But did all these words matter?

In the two years that passed between one sentence and the next, her friend G. was arrested while performing illegal work in Germany and shot at Brandenburg Prison, and her lovely friend Z. was behind bars. She'd heard that poet J.—cat hair on his jacket, his teeth brown from smoking—had gone underground, but she never heard from him again.

Certainly all decisions about whom one should form alliances with—when and at what cost—had to be reevaluated moment by moment. Before you set out to fight the enemy, you had to know who the enemy was. But who could know for sure?

G. had long since been buried in Brandenburg soil, his two eyes shut forever—the Nazis had condemned and executed him on charges of high treason. If he were still alive, they would no doubt be charging him with high treason here in Moscow as well, since to the end he maintained a close friendship with A., the latter-day Trotskyite. Given that Hitler seemed not to be going anywhere and the formation of factions was proving to be part of the general collapse, this friendship (which at the time was not yet a crime but only something difficult to understand: an error perhaps, a case of thickheadedness, shortsighted obstinacy, but also perhaps, who knows, the result of meticulous tactical deliberations on the part of the *intellectual pioneer of the Communist movement G.)* would most certainly have metamorphosed into an unpardonable wrong. But by executing G. for treason in 1934 at Brandenburg Prison, the Fascists had ensured that what would remain in his comrades' memory was his fame. *Death is the beginning of immortality.* Meanwhile, the doors to the hall of fame have been sealed up, and the Beyond is nothing more than an endless strip of sand between the fronts, a no-man's-land in which all those who have gone missing over the last few months—now including her husband—will be forced, dead or alive, to walk on and on unto all eternity on their bloody feet.

She, too, had been acquainted with A., the latter-day so-called Trotskyite, ever since the first time she participated in a meeting of the Communist cell *Vienna-Margareten*, and she'd run into him a few times after his expulsion from the Party in 1926, the last time in Prague, shortly before she left for Moscow. This portly comrade had come late to a meeting of Austrian emigrants and had taken the last remaining empty chair, right next to hers, then he had spent the entire evening silently smoking, only once addressing her in a low voice, asking what had become of their mutual friend G. G. had recently been sent to Berlin, she'd replied, that's all she knew. I understand, the so-called Trotskyite had responded. The smoke of his cigarette had hovered above him, motionless and thick, and for a moment the smell reminded her of J., the poet who'd gone underground. When they were all saying their goodbyes outside afterward, she had impulsively hugged A., whom no one else was deigning to so much as shake hands with, but it seemed to her that he returned the hug more out of exhaustion than friendship.

I committed a serious error in November 1934. In Prague I participated in a meeting of Austrian Schutzbund supporters at which the Trotskyite A. was also present, and I did not report this to the Party organization. I was severely chastised for this by the Party leadership, but the reprimand was removed from my record after conversations with Comrades Sch. and K. when I practiced honest self-criticism with regard to my lack of vigilance.

Was it better to call an error you had recognized by its name, thereby taking away the power with which, years later, it threatened to destroy you? And did not the forcefulness of an error's attack fundamentally reflect the passion with which you had once committed it—in other words, was it you yourself creating your own downfall without knowing how and when?

Should she even mention that her self-criticism had been accepted? Did the expunged punishment require her report? Surely there were papers covering all of this, other people's reports. Surely she was mentioned in one or the other self-criticism written by someone else, or in the account of someone else's life. So should she simply leave unmentioned what had been expunged? But that might be interpreted as malicious concealment on her part. Should she drag this expunged punishment back out into the light? (But then it wouldn't be expunged any longer, would it?) It was a matter of honesty, such honesty as left each individual lying there as if naked before the other. But who would this other be? And what is the deepest layer one can lay bare? In the end, does coming clean mean scraping the very flesh from your bones?

And then, what are bones?

At the beginning of the 1920s they had studied the movements of money in their evening gatherings, its way of fluttering about, and the arbitrary power it was gaining over humankind.

Today, inflation can destroy a person more thoroughly than an *E. coli* infection, G. had said.

Then, fifteen years later, something began to flutter about and gain power over humankind, something that none of her friends and neither her husband nor she herself could put a name to. Had the time so quickly come to an end when words themselves were

144

reality, just as real as a bag of flour, a pair of shoes, or a crowd being stirred to revolt? Was it the case now that reality itself consisted of words? Whose eyes would piece together the letters she was writing into words, and the words into meaning? What would be called her guilt, her innocence? Did every word matter? What are bones?

Ever since her husband's arrest, she has felt like a stranger in this land, even though when they first arrived, it was a homecoming, despite the fact that they'd never set foot here before 1935. A homecoming to the future that was to belong to them. *Our metro,* she and her husband said when they saw the newly opened underground stations for the first time, *our Gastronom No. 1,* when they went shopping for the first time in this gigantic grocery store, where there were thirty-six kinds of cheese, and a stunning cornucopia of foodstuffs of all sorts, items whose names had been all but forgotten in Vienna and Prague; the saleswomen wore little white bonnets, and they didn't touch the cheese, meat, sausages, bread, or vegetables with their hands, but only with forks or rubber gloves. *Touching the merchandise is strictly prohibited.* To be sure, there were still small old shops where one could find flour being sold in hand-twisted sacks made of newsprint, here and there the customs of a bygone, unsanitary age still survived, but they would soon no doubt disappear amid the gleam of modernity. Once she had even sent her mother a package containing cheese, goose fat, caviar, sausages and bonbons. Let her mother see that she, the wayward daughter, had done everything right after all. Anything flourishing in the Soviet Union was flourishing in her own life as well. Her mother thanked her in a letter, asking how things were with her. And she had been proud to be able to write in her response: very good. A time comes when a daughter shouldn't have to give any other reply to her mother's question as to how she is doing. The *very good* will now remain with her forever, come what may. Her husband is *very good,* she writes when her mother asks her whether

145

H., too, is keeping well: for a person who doesn't know the truth, it makes no difference whether someone has been arrested or is just far, far away. *Very good*, she writes, when her mother asks her about her apartment and work. The reality behind this *very good* has gradually shifted, but that is nothing her mother needs to know. It is only a pity that her father, who was always on her side, did not live to see her time of happiness.

When the passport of a German friend expired, he couldn't get his residency permit extended. He was invited to visit the German embassy in Moscow to have his passport renewed. Invited to present himself to the Fascists who had him on a list, invited to turn himself in. He died not quite two months later at a concentration camp outside Weimar. He passed the test. Another comrade went to the German embassy and emerged with a new passport. He was received by the NKVD and shot as a German spy. He did not pass the test. Both are dead.

After Hitler's seizure of power I came to Prague. I have to say that I was profoundly depressed at the time. Never before in my life had I left German soil. It was very hard for me to say goodbye. I know that all I wanted was to get back to Germany as quickly as possible. I even considered wearing a disguise. Of course that would have been madness. In night after night of discussion, Comrade F. convinced me to go to Moscow. But I find it difficult to write here. In point of fact, we were rejected by Germany and don't yet have roots in the Soviet Union.

Her passport, too, has been a German passport ever since the *Anschluss*. Her passport, too, expired three weeks ago. Three times now the Soviet official she handed her document to for inspection took one look at it and slammed his window down in her face. Without a valid passport there's no extending her residency permit, no *propusk*, but she needs one in order to be allowed to go on living in her apartment. At least the building superintendent is still letting her go upstairs to her apartment at night, when no one will see, but it won't be long before the apartment is assigned to someone else. And then where will she go?

While she is writing the account of her life, she listens for the sound of the elevator. The day the elevator stops on her floor at around four or five in the morning—that will be the end. During the day, she sits in the coffeehouse Krasni Mak, red poppy, translating poems from Russian to German for her own edification. Without a *propusk*, there's no getting a work permit either. The money she has left from her husband will be enough, if she spends it frugally, for the next two weeks at most. Then what?

At night, instead of sleeping, she works on the account of her life, which she is using to apply for Soviet citizenship. But what if there is no right answer on this test? Will there eventually be only a single thing left to feel sure of: that each of the comrades dying, here or in Germany, has finally reached his goal, while each who has survived all of this, here or in Germany, purchased his life with treason?

Sometimes she would take her father's glasses off his nose to clean them. She and her friend had sometimes stood side by side, comparing their legs. Once she had lain awake all night long beside her friend's fiancé, weeping. For Comrade G. she had sliced through an entire stack of paper at one go. Before she kissed her husband for the first time, she had grabbed him by his shock of hair, pulling him toward her. Was she ever even the same person? Were there any two moments in her life when she was comparable to herself? Was the whole not the truth? Or was everything treason? If the person who is to read this account remains faceless to her, what face should she be showing him? Which is the right blank face for a blank mirror?

4

My husband was arrested on October 25, 1938.

Comrade Sch. in his yellow suit jacket always used to say contemptuously when two comrades fell in love: *They're privatizing.* France, England, and America had meanwhile recognized Hitler's government. If a person was now in love with the wrong idea, this put him objectively—whether he saw it this way or not—on the side of the Fascists. Friendship, love, and marriage were indeed a sticky subject in times when all signs were pointing to war.

Today we know that enemies of the people have slandered upstanding comrades in the name of political vigilance and brought about their arrests. I am convinced that the case of my husband H. is precisely such an instance and that his innocence will be demonstrated.

When she was a child, her father sometimes made faces for her in the dark, and precisely because she loved him so much, she was never entirely sure that her father was still her father at these times. She had always considered it possible that he might at any moment be transformed from the person she knew so well into something deadly, and then this deadliness would prove to be his actual nature. Just a single moment of truth like this could reveal his entire life to have been dissimulation.

Hadn't she sat in church on Sunday, a good Christian girl, while the next day, people might perhaps be spitting at her Jewish grandmother when she went to do her shopping at the Naschmarkt?

She'd reproached herself as a duplicitous wretch when she betrayed her best friend with her desires. Always there had been these dependencies, always the fear of desiring too much or not being good enough, leading to lies, to dissimulation, to silence. *Redhead, redhead, ding-a-ling, fire burns in Ottakring,* always the fear of giving too much of oneself or too little, *Jewish sow,* always the rungs separating human beings, the inferiorities, always someone pushing someone else downstairs, someone falling, knocking over the person below. Had not they, the Communists, made it their business to even out the gradient so that everyone could stand freely without falling, without pushing, shoving, being pushed or shoved, free—and without fear?

Never did anyone display a more upright and incorruptible character than my husband. In the three years we spent in the Soviet Union, H.'s every thought was devoted to working in the service of Socialism, combating Fascism, helping the Party.

Only after she had fallen in love with him had she realized what a great longing she'd always had to be knowable to another person: to be one with herself, and at the same time with another. Everything within her that she had secretly identified as wrong, all the trespasses she had committed, imagined, inherited, or desired—he'd laughed away all her shame and, with it, her susceptibility to blackmail. Love had meant saying what was in her heart, and this saying meant freedom, and for the first time her fear of not being good enough had gone away.

And hadn't Lenin's principle of criticism and self-criticism within the Party originally presupposed—and also set as its goal—absolute equality among all comrades and their mutual trust? Was it not this principle that was to facilitate growth? The more radically the individual set his own limitations aside, the more firmly the whole cohered. Why had G., then, whom she had always referred to as her *clever friend*, not sacrificed his friendship with A.?

Truly we are coming to know one another in the course of these exchanges, we see each other quite clearly. This is my profound insight, what I understand here as a Bolshevik, what I experience: Bolshevism's power, its intellectual power, is so strong that it forces us to speak the truth. As

Communists we should show our faces, in other words show the entire person. You can't just say that you didn't have time to be vigilant because you had to bring money to your wife at your dacha. When we have been successful in creating a clean atmosphere, we will truly be able to work cleanly and productively.

Until recently, she'd shared her husband's view that it was crucial they scrutinize their own ranks closely to keep the core stable. She'd reclined on the sofa as he sat in an armchair, reading to her from the thick volume containing the latest report on the court proceedings. After Radek, Zinoviev, Kamenev—the original revolutionaries, once lauded as *Lenin's stalwart brothers-in-arms*—Bukharin, too, had made a public confession, declaring himself guilty of conspiracy and treason, and he had been condemned to death and shot. In his last plea, he'd said: *When you ask yourself, "If you must die, what are you dying for?"—suddenly a pitch-black void appears before you with shocking clarity. There is nothing worth dying for if you want to die unrepentant.* He'd taken this opportunity to declare his loyalty to the Soviet Union one last time.

She and her husband had met Bukharin right at the beginning of their time in Moscow. The very day they arrived, he had telephoned the hotel of the Austrian and German comrades who'd just escaped from their own countries—countries where they'd been in hiding—and personally delivered a piece of bread and bacon to each of their rooms.

Now, would she still have a chance to describe the sound the pages of the thick book made as they turned? Page after page, she heard in her husband's voice the way these living beings were transformed into ghosts.

Only now that she is alone has she begun to ask herself if it is really necessary to radically cut away everything that is weak or gravitates to the fringes. The core of a sphere, her little sister would probably say (she who was always so good at math), is basically just a point, but one whose size approaches infinity on the negative axis. But what was the core? An idea? An individual? Could it be Stalin? Or the utterly disembodied, utterly pure belief in a better world? And whose head was this belief supposed to inhabit if the day came when not a single head remained? An individual could lose his head, she'd thought two years ago, but not an entire Party. Now it was looking as if an entire Party really could lose all its individual heads, as if the sphere itself were spinning all its points away from it, becoming smaller and smaller, just to reassure itself that its center held firm. Approaching infinity on the negative axis.

In Vienna her husband used to laugh whenever a theater critic wrote: *He wasn't playing Othello—he was Othello. Old-fashioned* was his word for this mania for perfect illusions. He interpreted the flawless melding of actor and mask as the pinnacle of bourgeois deceit, and now, in the Land of the Future—where the labor of all for all supposedly had been stripped of deception, where individual gain resulted in profit for all, while egotism and tactical maneuvering could be eliminated before they arose—he himself stood accused of duplicity? Had they, as people on the run, changed their names so often their own comrades had lost all memory of what lay behind the names? Why else was there so much talk of costumes and masks? Or had they, locked in battle with an external enemy, begun to turn into this enemy without realizing it? Would this new thing hatching out of them bear them ill will? Had their own growing gone over to the other side unbeknownst to them?

The head of any dialectically functional human being contains all thoughts. It's just a question of which thought I let out. Obviously man is guilty. Yet the thought also arises that man is innocent. I cannot escape this dilemma by constantly harping on the young poet D., who is innocent. It keeps coming down to the same thing: on one hand, innocent D., and on the other a random arrest. The man is innocent, and I see that he is innocent, I try to help prove his innocence, and then he is arrested, and this means that the arrest was random. But since an arrest is never random, it is therefore proven that the man is not innocent. Therefore I am willing to concede the point to you, in a case where you are in the wrong.

On this bit of steppe, 45.61404 degrees latitude north, 70.751954 degrees longitude east, there are only three months a year without frost. In only a few weeks, the grass will lose this green tint it displays, it will turn brown, and when the wind blows one stalk against the other, it will rustle faintly. Before the first snow falls, tiny ice crystals will cover the blades, and even the little stones on the surface of the steppe will without exception be covered with hoarfrost and freeze together. Once the frost sets in, it will no longer be possible for the wind to blow the stones about.

The weekend before his arrest, her husband had gone to a meeting and, upon returning, in distinct contrast to his usual habit, had said nothing at all about what had been discussed there. It was nearly dawn when he got home, and he did not laugh away her fears, baring his teeth and flipping back his strand of hair; she had seen him this tight-lipped only once before, that time two years earlier when he had learned that his application for membership in the Communist Party of the Soviet Union had been approved, but hers had not.

Now that her husband has been taken away, she knows that when she sits here putting her life to paper, she is playing not just with her own life, but with his as well, not just with her own death, but also with his; or is she playing against death—or does all this pro and contra make no difference at all? She knows that with every word she writes or leaves unwritten she is playing with the lives of her friends, just as her friends in turn, when they are asked about her, are forced to play with hers. G., *the intellectual pioneer of the Commu-*

nist movement, had to the bitter end refused to sacrifice his friendship with the Trotskyist A.

> *I understand that Comrade H. has been living for approximately three years together with his wife, Comrade H., in Moscow. He met her before this, but three years ago is when they entered into wedlock. Did Comrade H. question other comrades with regard to his wife's earlier life, or was she his only source of information?*
>
> *My wife, Comrade H., as many of you know, has been a member of the Communist Party of Austria since 1920.*
>
> *Immediately before her departure to Moscow, she had contact in Prague with the Trotskyite A.*
>
> *I can't respond to that, I was still in Berlin at the time.*
>
> *We have not only the right but also the duty to speak about everything we know.*
>
> *Only in his later work did A. develop Trotskyist tendencies. I can assure you that Comrade H. did not identify with him and, above all, where his assessment of the Soviet Union was concerned, she vehemently disagreed.*
>
> *It seems to me her relationship with A. went beyond mere friendship. In any case, the two of them embraced when they parted on the evening in question, according to the report of Comrade Sch.*
>
> *I can't respond to that.*
>
> *Answer this question: Could Trotskyite, semi-Trotskyite, or oppositional leanings be observed in her?*
>
> *No, not at that time.*
>
> *What does "not at that time" mean? I have to say I don't have the impression that this testimony is completely truthful. What's hiding behind it? Why does Comrade H. not speak freely about the case of his wife Comrade H. in this context? Why does he have to be prompted by additional questions to speak of it?*
>
> *There was no question of any opposition on her part in the sense in which we use this term in the Party.*

153

I hope that it is clear to all our comrades how crucial it is for us to spare no effort in critical situations. These criminals who have been torturing our comrades in Germany and sending us their spies must be met with wave after wave of destruction. What if scoundrels or counterrevolutionaries like A. had managed to point a gun at Comrade Stalin? Comrades, we are faced with the question: peace or war?

Would her motherly friend O.—with whom they shared a dacha summer after summer, often staying on into September—conceal or admit under interrogation that they had all expressed doubts regarding the guilt of the young poet D. after his arrest? Might the wife of the author V. (V. had been recently condemned on charges of engaging in Trotskyist activities and shot), who was now supporting herself as a seamstress and had come to her room for a fitting, really have dug around in her papers when she stepped out to the toilet? Why had R., with whom she and her husband had enjoyed so many excellent conversations about literature early in their Moscow days, been sent off to an outpost in the German Volga Republic exactly one week before her husband's arrest? Who was responsible for cutting the final sentence of the review she had written in July for the *Deutsche Zentral-Zeitung* so that her critique of the book by mustached K. was transformed into its opposite? And was that good or bad fortune? She's long since stopped getting together with the friends she used to play cards with sometimes in those first years after they arrived, and the literary working groups were dissolved two years ago. Even the assemblies of German Party members have been discontinued. Her friend C., who used to cry her eyes out in front of her all the time over her inability to have children, recently refused to so much as nod in greeting when she walked past Café Krasni Mak and saw her—*the wife of H., who has been arrested*—sitting at the window.

And she herself?

During the rehearsals for the last play her husband wrote before his arrest, five of the eight actors were arrested over a period of several days, after which rehearsals were canceled until further notice. Comrade Fr., the wife of one of these actors, came up to her yesterday at the café, holding the hand of Sasha, her nine-year-old son, and entreated her to take the two of them in for at least a night. I can't, she responded. Without another word, the woman turned and went out again, holding her child by the hand. I can't. Only a few weeks before, her husband had been folding paper airplanes for Sasha during breaks in rehearsal. It seems to her unimaginably long ago now that she learned from the poet Mayakovski: *It is not enough to be eighteen years old.*

In their fight against the Fascists' despotism and contempt for human dignity, they had all risked their lives, wrestling with the death that is fascism, and many of them fell victim to it. But if the young, beautiful Soviet Union was, by contrast, Life itself (as she believes even now), then death could no longer serve as a currency here. This fmeant that if even only a single person who fought against despotism lost his life to despotism here, then his death was in vain—deeply, profoundly, in vain—and nothing that remained here deserved the name Life, even if, seen from the outside, it resembled life.

But if in the land of the future, death were still the currency with which you paid a debt you didn't know you had—in other words if it hadn't been possible even here to abolish the rift between human beings that goes by the names trade, commerce, and deception, if even here there were still the same accursed two sides to humanity, unbridgeable, just as in any transaction in the old world, that would mean the sale had already gone through, and all her comrades—including her and her husband—were long since betrayed and sold and now served only to bring the seller a good price: one consisting of themselves, paid not just once or twice or even three times, but ten, a hundred, perhaps even a thousand times over.

★

So have things really come so far now that all she can do is hope
that the members of the secret police who seized her husband and
took him away *in the name of political vigilance* are merely traitors,
enemies of the people, that they are Hitler's people—possibly even
high-ranking ones? Not only her husband but in fact every last one
of the comrades whose arrests she's been hearing about is someone
she's known well for years. She's now almost certain: if Hitler himself proves to be her adversary even here in the capital of the Soviet
Union, only then can the antifascists' hope for a better world possibly survive their torture and death. Or is it perhaps that Stalin himself—disguised as Hitler, who in turn is disguised as Stalin, doubly
masked, doubly veiled, and thus genuinely duplicitous—that Stalin himself is acting as his own agent and, out of fear that in a good
world the hope for a better one might be lost forever, out of fear
of stagnation, is now trying to murder the Communist movement
back into hopefulness? Or perhaps that all of them together are
dreaming a nightmare from which there will never be an awaken-
ing, and in this nightmare Stalin, the good father, creeps into the
rooms where his children are sleeping with a knife in his hands.

Land of ours that blooms and blossoms,
Listen, darling, listen,
Was given to us for time eternal.
Hear me, darling, listen.

Child, thy land is guarded well,
Sleep, my angel, slumber.
Red Army men watch over you.
Sleep, my darling, slumber.

5

When she gets up again to fetch more hot water from the samovar in the common kitchen for her tea, she runs into Indian comrade Al in the hallway. He greets her but today he doesn't initiate a conversation. No doubt he, too, has heard about her husband's arrest. Last month, when he was still new in Moscow, she and her husband had gotten into conversation with him while they were cooking, first he had leaned up against the kitchen table, still standing, then at some point hopped up on the table's edge, his legs dangling, and finally he'd drawn his legs up beneath him, still talking, like a very-much-alive Buddha sitting there on this worn-out tabletop where the Russians had no doubt cut their *pelmeni* in the age of the Czars, and later Chinese comrades had rolled hard-boiled duck eggs in ashes, and Frenchmen dipped meat in a marinade of garlic and oil. She herself, on the occasion of the Seventh World Congress two years before, had used this table to make apple strudel for her Danish, Polish, and American friends. This congress had been like a powerful amorous coupling, all of them melting into one another, conjoined in their common battle for a humanity finally coming to its senses. After these meetings, she and her husband would often go on deliberating deep into the night, lying in bed, discussing what this new world order should look like, whether it was still an order at all, and what new bonds should replace the old bonds of coercion.

> Then L. shoved his way in and started shouting at me. I told him to shut up, then he pushed me over to the side and started grabbing at the front of my shirt.
> M. says I grabbed hold of him by the shirt. Everyone knows this is untrue. I've never grabbed anyone's shirt, what an idea!

There were eight comrades standing around. I said to L., Don't touch me.
L. shouted back, Don't touch me. So then I repeated, Take your paws
off me.
All of a sudden Comrade M. said, Get your stinking paws off me.
Then L started saying, You'll be sorry you did that, I'm going to report
you to a Party cell.
Then M. shouted, Maybe they'll wash your stinking paws in innocence
for you!
Comrade L. has a booming voice, and he really let rip: Just you wait and
see what I do with people like you!
Ridiculous!

In the room she has shared with her husband for the past three
years, in whose emptiness she is now setting foot once more, the
yellow wall hanging with the embroidered sun from their first Soviet vacation still hangs on the wall. Every morning she leaves the
house before dawn and gets in line in front of Lubyanka 14—the
headquarters of the secret police—to ask about her husband; and
after this, she goes to Butyrka Prison. In both places the counter
clerks slam down their windows in her face. She has already written
to Pieck, to Dimitrov, Ulbricht, and Bredel, but no one is able or
willing to give her any information as to whether her husband will
return, whether his arrest was a mistake, whether he's being put on
trial, whether they're planning to send him into exile, or shoot him.
Or whether he's already been shot. Suddenly she remembers how
her friend's lover sat beside her that night, his tears dripping quietly to the floor before his feet. Only now does she know as much
about life as he knew then. With the arrest of the person who was
closer to her than any other, her own life has become fundamentally inaccessible to her.

I petition you for acceptance into the Soviet Federation and request that
you give me the opportunity to prove myself as a Soviet.

6

When the elevator stops on her floor at around four in the morning, just before sunrise, she doesn't hear it, because she has fallen asleep over the papers on her desk. Her forehead is resting on the word *vigilance* when the officers come into the room to arrest her. The small dark-blue suitcase that has long stood in readiness beside the door is forgotten. When silence returns to the building, the suitcase is still standing there beside the door. It contains a photograph of a young woman with a large hat, stamped on the back by the owner of a photography studio on Landstrasser Hauptstrasse in Vienna; further, a notebook filled with writing, several letters, an Austrian passport, a dirty red handbill, membership papers for the Communist Party of Austria, a handwritten excerpt concerning "Earthquakes in Styria," a typescript wrapped in paper, a recipe for challah, and at the very bottom, a small dress for a doll, sloppily and shoddily sewn of pink silk.

And now at last she knows whose voices she has been hearing all this time, she encounters them once more at minus sixty-three degrees Celsius. How agreeable it is to be without a body in cold like this. At night in this place far beyond the end of the world, ores are separated from their slag, everything worthless is incinerated, blazing up in flames higher than St. Stephen's Cathedral: brilliantly colorful formations, bright as the horizon itself, fountains of light more beautiful than anything she has ever seen before, how glorious, this burning of slag in the middle of nowhere, the most beautiful of all things ever.

During the day, the living hack away at the ore-rich clay, carting it off in their tipping wagons, and at night they set these fires. And in these fires, all the sentences the dead spoke back when they themselves were still alive are incinerated—sentences spoken in fear, out of conviction, in anger, out of indifference, or love. Why are you here? she asks a person she knows once uttered the words: *We see each other quite clearly in the course of these exchanges.* I was thirsty, he says, so I drank water that hadn't been boiled and died of typhus. And you? she asks a person she knows once referred to a mutual colleague as a *writer of trash.* I froze to death. And you? *What if someone sees us?* that person had asked. I died of hunger. Some sentence flies up to the sky, possessing no more, no less weight than the person who once spoke it. And you? I went mad, and only death brought me back to my senses, he says, laughing, and here, seven hundred feet above the steppe, his laughter has a furry consistency. Another bit of air says, All I remember is leaning up against something because I was too weak to go on walking, and someone looked into my eyes as he walked past, since I still had eyes. I'm glad, she hears a woman's voice saying—hears without ears, just as she sees without eyes—I'm glad, she hears the voice saying, that my tears finally abandoned me along with my eyes, because when I was arrested, my own child renounced me, calling me an *enemy of the people,* and so I tore up my shirt, twisted it into a noose, and hung myself from a latch.

We see each other quite clearly in the course of these exchanges.

Perhaps someone should investigate the strength of the draft created when a soul flits about like this. Perhaps someday flowers will bloom even here, in the middle of the wasteland, perhaps even tulips, perhaps someday the presence of innumerable butterflies will be just as real as the absence of butterflies of any sort today, at minus sixty-three degrees Celsius. Now, like all the rest of the dead, she has all the time in the world to wait for the arrival of different times. For the living, to be sure—who have no other time at their disposal than the one in which they happen to possess a body—the only bit of color they're able to behold here at night, together with the dead, are these flames.

7

Last summer, when she was still alive, she, along with the other women, had to dig several large trenches just outside the camp, so when winter came and the ground froze, they would have somewhere to be buried. All of them—she and her friends, her enemies, and also those who were indifferent to them—they all dug graves to be kept in reserve.

On one particular day during the summer of '41, she drove her pickaxe into the earth at a specific point and began to dig her own grave, without knowing, of course, that this was the exact place on all this infinite earth destined to become her dwelling for the eternal winter. The coordinates 45.61404 degrees latitude north and 70.75195 degrees longitude east would be what people would use to describe this otherwise nameless place, where on a summer's day, at forty degrees Celsius, she would drive her pickaxe into the dry sand, making grass, tiny insects, and dust fly around, for the earth here was completely dry far down into its depths.

How lovely is your dwelling place, oh Lord of Hosts.

One night during the winter of '41, while everyone was asleep, the woman on duty pulled the cold right leg of a dead woman out from beneath the warm leg of a sleeping woman, she dragged the lifeless body out of the barrack, and brought it to the barrack for the dead. At such temperatures it takes less than two days for a body like this, including all the flesh covering its bones, to freeze into a skeleton.

Many years ago one person said a word, and then another said another word, words moved the air, words were written down on paper with ink and clipped into binders. Air was balanced out with air, and ink with ink. It's a shame that no one can see the boundary where words made of air and words made of ink are transformed into something real: as real as a bag of flour, a crowd in which revolt is stirring, just as real as the sound with which the frozen bones of Comrade H. slid down into a pit in the winter of '41, sounding like someone tossing wooden domino tiles back into their box. When it's cold enough, something that was once made of flesh and blood can sound just like wood.

INTERMEZZO

Comrade Ö., who always used to refer privately—i.e. in conversation with his wife—to Comrade H. as a *narrow-lipped hysteric*, places her dossier on the left-hand stack on his desk, not the stack to his right.

The stack on the left is forwarded to Comrade B.

Comrade B., opening the file, remembers that he once visited H. and his wife at their dacha many years ago and that the wife had baked an excellent apple strudel. But an apple strudel cannot be sufficient grounds for sparing a counterrevolutionary element. For this reason he places the dossier on the left-hand stack, not the stack to his right.

The stack on the left is forwarded to Comrade S.

Comrade S. wonders whether, if Comrade H. were to be arrested—and was she still a comrade to begin with?—she might say something disadvantageous about him in the hope of saving her own skin. Had he ever said anything to her that might somehow incriminate him? Since he cannot remember anything of the sort, he places her file on the left-hand stack on his desk, not the stack to his right.

The stack on the left is forwarded to Comrade L.

Comrade L. reads the account Comrade H. has written of her life, which is included in her dossier, up to the point where it becomes clear that the Comrade H. who was recently arrested is her husband. This H. once literally accused him during a debate of *having no balls*. For this reason, without hesitation, he places the account of the life of Comrade H.—the wife of Comrade H. and someone he never actually met in person—back in her dossier, he closes it and places it on the left-hand stack on his desk, not the stack to his right.

The stack on the left is forwarded to Comrade F.

Comrade F. knows Comrade H. quite well, and also knows her husband, who has already been arrested. He considers it utterly implausible that the two of them could be Trotskyist spies as has been alleged. The stack on the right-hand side of his desk already contains five dossiers of good friends on whose behalf he means to intercede directly with Stalin. More than five can't possibly work, of this he's quite aware.

He gets up and takes a bottle of vodka from the shelf. While he is filling his glass all the way to the rim, placing it against his lower lip and knocking it back, he thinks about how during one of the last Writers Union debates he was described as a *hopeless drunk*.

He goes back to his desk and places the dossier of Comrade H. to the left. Later he forwards all the files from the left-hand stack to his Soviet Comrade Shu.

Soviet Comrade Shu. is required—according to NKVD Order No. 00439, Order No. 00485 and other orders relating to national arrest quotas—to make fifty arrests from each of the following groups: Germans, Poles, Koreans, Greeks, and Iranians by the end of this month, October 1938. To assemble these lists, he proceeds alphabetically, in other words begins with the letter A. for each nationality.

Working through the Iranian contingent, he gets to the letter N.

With the Greeks, to S.

With the Koreans, to L.

With the Poles to D.

And with the Germans to F.

As he is preparing these lists, he makes a minor error, confusing the name Comrade H. used to enter the Soviet Union with her real name. In the fake German passport she used to enter the Soviet Union four years ago, her name was Lisa Fahrenwald, F. for short.

But she's still lucky to have wound up at the end of the list, because the first ten persons in each contingent fall into Category 1. For Category 1 the sentence is: *death by firing squad*.

But for Category 2—in other words, for the remaining forty persons on each list, including H., who figures here mistakenly under the name Lisa Fahrenwald—the sentence is only: *prison camp, eight to ten years*.

But things might also have gone quite differently.

Comrade Ö., who always used to refer to Comrade H. privately—i.e. in conversation with his wife—as a *narrow-lipped hysteric*, would still have placed her dossier on the left-hand stack on his desk, not the stack to his right. And the stack on the left would still have been forwarded to Comrade B.

But if Comrade B. had, for example, not only remembered Comrade H.'s excellent apple strudel but also stopped to consider that if she were to be interrogated, she would quite likely mention him as an acquaintance if not a friend on the basis of his visit to their dacha; he would probably have found it advisable to place her dossier on the right-hand stack.

But if this thought had not occurred to him, if Comrade H.'s dossier had remained there on the left-hand stack, then after the file was forwarded, Comrade S. might perhaps have remembered that right after the assembly that past March at which their Party group had responded to Bukharin's conviction, he had been standing with Comrade H. and his wife and in a moment of high spirits he'd told a political joke.

Three prisoners are sitting in a cell and they get to talking.
Why are you in prison?

I was for Bukharin.
What about you?
I was against Bukharin.
And you?
I am Bukharin.

The three of them had shared a laugh. But what if Comrade H.—was she still a comrade to begin with?—happened to remember during an interrogation that he had told this joke, that would certainly be his downfall. And so Comrade S. would have chosen the right-hand stack and not the one to his left.

Only if his memory had failed him would the file marked H. still have wound up on the left-hand stack and been forwarded to Comrade L.

Comrade L. might, who knows, suddenly have started musing while he was flipping through the file: Wasn't this H. the woman whose splendid red hair he had often admired from afar during assemblies without ever having been introduced to her? He would casually have asked his secretary, who was just coming in with more files, if she knew what H. looked like, and his secretary would have said: Oh, one of those Jewish carrot-tops. Hereupon, and after the secretary's departure, he would have placed the account of H.'s life on the right-hand stack.

Although she was apparently the wife of Comrade H., who once publicly accused him of *having no balls*.

But as far as he knew, H. had been arrested.

After this he would have paused for a moment before continuing to sort the files and tried to imagine what H., the *Jewish carrot-top* with the milky skin, might look like between her legs—was her hair down there red as well, or maybe blond?

But if, for example, his secretary had *not* come into the room just at the moment when Comrade L. was holding H.'s dossier in his hands, the file would most probably have wound up on the left-hand stack on Comrade L.'s desk and been forwarded to Comrade F.

Now Comrade F. knows Comrade H. quite well, and also knows her husband, who has already been arrested. He considers it utterly implausible that the two of them could be Trotskyist spies as has been alleged. The stack on the right-hand side of his desk already contains five dossiers of good friends on whose behalf he means to intercede directly with Stalin. More than five can't possibly work, of this he's quite aware.

Perhaps he gets up and takes a bottle of vodka from the shelf. And thinks, as he fills his glass all the way to the rim, places it against his lower lip, and knocks it back, how during one of the last Writers Union debates he was described as a *hopeless drunk*.

Perhaps he goes back to his desk, looks through the files of his friends once more, finally taking one of them and placing it on the other stack, to his left, while placing H.'s file on the stack to the right.

And a short time later, he forwards only the files from the left-hand stack to his Soviet Comrade Shu.

And if not? What if he didn't trade H. for one of his five friends but instead passed her on to Comrade Shu.?

Then Comrade Shu. might, upon making a careful study of H.'s file, have been able or, indeed, compelled to see that Lisa Fahrenwald—F. for short—was actually Comrade H., and so she would not have been included in the contingent of German comrades on this day, neither in Category 1 nor in Category 2.

One week later, when it was time for letters H. through M. to be arrested, H. would—exceptionally—have been spending the night at the home of her old friend O. after running into her by chance at Café Krasni Mak and talking about her loneliness, something she was only able to discuss openly with a friend she had known so many years.

I've never been so lonely in all my life since they arrested H., she would have told her friend. At this, O. would have taken her by the arm and led her out of the café, she would have strolled with her down Arbat all the way to the apartment house where her room was. Late at night, H. would have told her friend about nine-year-old Sasha and the paper airplanes and begun to cry. Hereupon O. would have put a mattress on the floor for her in the alcove of her tiny room and kept her friend H. with her overnight.

For this reason, the NKVD officials would not have found her at home that night, the night when it was the turn of the letter H., and that was that; the following week, it would already have been the turn of the letter N, for example, Neuwiedner, and meanwhile Comrade H.'s application for Soviet citizenship would have been approved, forever removing her from Comrade Shu.'s jurisdiction.

By the end of 1938, the arrest of secret police chief Yezhov would have put an end to the era of the arrests of people by contingent, though many of those arrested under Yezhov would never reappear. Comrade H. would have written many more letters in an attempt to discover how and where her husband was, but not one of these letters would have ever been answered. She would have asked about him many more times, and many more times seen and heard one or another official slam his window peevishly down before her. Others fared better with their questions and learned at one or the other window that their husbands or sons were in a different prison, or already in exile, where, to be sure, they would possibly starve to death or freeze. Then they would start shouting or speaking entreatingly, while others just stood there quietly weeping, or fell silent altogether.

As for earning her living, she couldn't have taken work as a seamstress like the wife of V., who had also been arrested; it had been established once and for all that she was untalented in this regard, *sloppy* and *shoddy*. Nor could she apply to become a teacher at the Liebknecht German School in Moscow, since the school had been closed half a year before after the arrest of nearly its entire faculty. At the Marx-Engels Institute, Radio Moscow, the publishing house that printed German-language books in the Soviet Union, and even the *Deutsche Zentral-Zeitung*—everywhere, everyone knew that she was the wife of H., who'd been arrested.

She was most certainly not a whore.

Right?

For two pairs of shoes? One liter of cream? For fifteen potatoes or one half pound of fat?

Esteemed Comrade Dimitrov, please help me. Give me work. Don't let me drown.

Would it really be so awful to sell her body and its orifices for an hour or half an hour at a time to keep this body alive?

She would never have learned to whom, in the end, she owed the position she found herself being offered at the eleventh hour: translating Soviet poetry for the journal *Internationale Literatur*.

Where was a poem while it was being translated from one language to another? Only in the few hours she spent in this no-man's-land of words would she occasionally manage to think of something other than the man she loved and her misfortune.

She would have translated—for starvation wages, but still—and the Germans would have started the war, her husband would have remained missing, and sometimes she would have washed windows here and there to earn a little on the side, and the Germans would have attacked the Soviet Union despite the Non-aggression Pact, and even now her husband would not have returned home, the Germans would have bombed Kiev, and she would have waited and waited, and Dimitrov would have offered to let her write for the underground radio station *Institut 101*, there would have been air raids over Moscow, and she would have written for the radio, and Moscow would have used boards and paint as camouflage, making itself unrecognizable to the Germans—she spoke German—they had covered up the Moskva with boards as though it were no longer a river, and whitewashed the walls of the Kremlin to look like ordinary apartment buildings, making the golden cupolas suddenly

171

green, at night the air-raid alerts sent her to the metro station, and then she would have gone on waiting until the beginning of October '41, and then at the radio station she would have encountered someone whose poems she knew and thought highly of.

So pleased to meet you.

You speak Russian very well.

Oh, I don't know.

Truly.

Someone who was a Soviet poet, and she'd have sworn he almost ... and with her body ... and he would have ... and then the two of them ... and then, oh ... simply given away, what? ... all her orifices, thinking constantly of her husband ... of course it was out of the question, certainly impossible ... and therefore at the crack of dawn, even before he ... and all this time there were air raids over Moscow, and later the doctor would have said: a kidney infection, and then she would have evacuated, Kursk Station: four suitcases, war, a train to Ufa. And only there, in the Urals, would she have, not a kidney infection but her sixth month, Moscow stands firm, and the Soviet poet has left for Tashkent, yes, well, the baby, a boy, never an opportunity to tell the poet, never any letters, she never saw him again; Comrade O. produced a cradle for the baby, she wrote more radio programs ... scorched earth ... writing German for Germans; never an opportunity to tell him, never any letters, he was never there. And her husband, H.? Writing to fend off the German Fascists ... never give the enemy a handhold, never overvalue the private fate of the individual ... nursed the child for a year and a half while others starved, H. lost forever? And then the breaking free: the immense exertion, the greater the sacrifice made for the cause, the more just the cause must be. The crying baby—truly, it should have been his child, the child of her H. A good article, genuinely important, antifascism and war, a genuinely good program, and her H., genuinely lost forever? A Russian *niania* for the baby ... how do you write your way into the hearts of the German Fascists ...

the battle of encirclement, Stalingrad stands firm ... and if you get in, turn their hearts around inside their bodies? Her child, at three, more Russian than German. And finally the war would have been over, back to Moscow with her four suitcases. And her beloved H. still lost forever in all likelihood, and the distant poet probably still writing poems, in Russian. And her child would have asked, in Russian, where the end of the world was. Her comrades' invitation, and she thought, why not back to Berlin if it came to that? Her letter to her mother had long since come back to her stamped *Evacuated to the East*, so she had no family left in Vienna, and probably nowhere else either. In all probability. So: Belorussky Station, to Berlin. Culture work. Rebuilding. And the child: he was still much too young for her to explain to him who his father, or who his real father— even this father too far away to tell him how his son, and that to begin with ... besides which, she never wrote any letters, not a single word. A new beginning. Rubble. *Sisyphus*, finally out of her suitcase and in print.

I want to see my friends!

Who are your friends?

The wolves, the foxes, and the ghosts!

At least he's still there in Tashkent, or where? The Soviet poet. Never again any news of H. Membership in the Socialist Unity Party. No opportunity to say, or write, and the child not yet able to understand. Her first play performed, a great success: esteemed Comrade H. Could her husband possibly still be alive after all?

Some day when I'm dead, my toys will still be here.

Spare the child all of that.

Your father fell at the Battle of Kharkov.

Or something like that.

Wolves, foxes, and ghosts.

Not one word more.

BOOK IV

We must bid farewell to Comrade H., who soon would have completed her sixth decade of life.

He points to one of the wreaths.

All her life she devoted her abilities to serving the working classes and her Party. In her we are losing an exemplary champion of proletarian-revolutionary art.

He writes the text that is to be printed on the ribbon: *For my mother.*

In black script or gold?

Black.

Born in Brody, the daughter of an Austrian civil servant, she grew up in Vienna and in 1920 became a member of the Communist Party. In 1933 she emigrated to Moscow by way of Prague. There she contributed to the understanding between peoples as a translator of Soviet poetry for the journal Internationale Literatur *and immediately after Hitler's treacherous attack on the Soviet Union began her active antifascist work for the underground radio station operated by Radio Moscow.*

Sure, he says, why not have rose petals to toss into the grave?

After returning from exile, she moved to Berlin and here, in her tireless efforts on behalf of world peace and Socialism, she began to publish her first autonomous literary works.

How many?

How many are there usually?

One basket, two baskets, five baskets—depends how many mourners you're expecting.

Let's make it five, he says.

Thereafter she made significant contributions to the development of art and culture in the GDR with her important novels, works for theater, stories, reportage and radio plays. This great artist was nearly unmatched in her ability to bring the attention of our People to the world's most righteous strivings.

2

As she falls, she knows that she is falling, she knows that the railing is already too far away to reach with her left hand (much less the right), and suddenly she remembers the railing on the stairs in Vienna and how huge the eagle at the end of the banister had looked to her as a girl, how the stairwell always smelled of whitewash and dust, all of this occurs to her as she falls, as if memory, too, were a form of falling. Now she really is a "fallen woman" for the first time in her life, and if it weren't less a laughing matter than a dying one, she'd have to laugh. Did her mother think of her in her final moments? *Is* this her final moment? Back when she heard Khrushchev's secret speech broadcast on a West Berlin radio station, she'd suffered a heart attack and survived, so how can she be on the point of death now just because she's been knocked literally off her feet between one step and the next? The first chapter a tragedy, the second always a farce—had she only read Marx so she'd understand now that this really was the end for her? How do you recognize your final moment? Is it that more thoughts can be thought in it than any other? What is this abyss gaping open before her and swallowing up all the thoughts a person can think, and where was it before? If she tumbles out of life, what will happen to her son?

3

On the morning his mother is incinerated, her son spends two hours at home sitting at the desk in the desk chair where his mother always sat when she was working, and he waits for the time to pass.

Her work was honored with many prestigious prizes and awards by our Republic, including the Comrade-G. Medal, the Great Patriotic Order of Merit, and the Goethe Prize.

The desk chair is covered with blue leatherette and can spin on its axis. Sometimes as a child he would sit on it, spinning in circles until he was dizzy. He doesn't think his mother ever used this chair to spin on.

Her work in defense of the beautiful and true is her legacy to us all and will inspire us in our struggle to achieve the reunification of our homeland and world peace.

4

Dear Mother, she had written near the end of the war, *things are very good with me. I have a son now, he is three years old and is named Sasha.* How long had it been since her mother had sent the little box with the gold buttons from her father's civil-service uniform to her in Moscow? And she hadn't even thanked her. She'd thought that her mother had just wanted to get rid of her last remaining souvenir of her husband, that her mother didn't know what it truly meant to love. Then, with the start of the war and her relocation to Ufa, her contact with Vienna had broken off. Only near the end of the war, in Moscow—when she learned through her work at the radio station what had been happening to the Jews in countries defeated by Germany—did she ask herself when her mother's package had arrived: in 1939 perhaps, or 1940? *Dear Mother, things are very good*

with me. I have a son now, he is three years old and is named Sasha. The
letter had come back to her stamped *Evacuated to the East.* And now,
sealed and multiply stamped as it had been when it was returned to
her, it lay at the very bottom of her linen cabinet, underneath the
sheets. Her son would find this letter sooner or later. Now, she has
no secrets left. She cannot protect her son any longer, nor herself.

5

The housekeeper found her at the foot of the stairs when she arrived that morning. At around 10:30—but perhaps it had happened
earlier—her son at school had just finished his essay on Goethe's
poem "*Willkommen und Abschied.*" The moment at which his entire
life changed did not look any different from all the other moments
before or after it. Probably, the housekeeper says, his mother had
just changed her clothes upstairs and wanted to go down to her
study. Those stairs are treacherous, the housekeeper says. As a small
child, he had only slid down the banister when his mother wasn't
looking. He could fall, could break a leg or his neck. *Do me a favor,
don't go falling down the stairs,* his mother always said. Certainly she
herself never went sliding down the banister, she always just walked
up, walked down, step after step—but the stairs are treacherous, as
the housekeeper says.

6

What actually happened to your relatives, her son had asked her
when he was already a bit older. There were air raids on Vienna, she
said. It would have been easier to answer questions about so many

other things, but he'd never asked about them. She would have liked to tell him what sort of apples she used for her strudel. Now she'd taken a tumble. Now she was falling down a flight of stairs, and these stairs no longer led to the ground floor of her house, no longer to her study, no longer to the front door, no longer to the kitchen; for her, since she believed in nothing supernatural, these stairs led only from the upper floor of her house down to nothingness. Never would she have thought that the border between what is and what isn't could gape open so abruptly.

Really? her little sister asks.

And that it has to happen right in the middle of life, on a stupid flight of stairs.

You were just plowing on ahead like always.

Don't be silly. I weigh too much, that's all.

It shows that things are good with you.

Never again permit myself to be blackmailed by hunger.

You won that one.

And now I'm going to die because I'm such a blimp.

Nonsense.

I go to a resort to take it off every year.

So as not to let yourself be blackmailed by food.

Once I lost twenty-six pounds.

That's quite a lot.

And now?

7

The housekeeper says she made sure that the men who came to get his mother were gentle with her. One of her legs had gotten caught in the railing, and she was lying head-down, but that's all the detail she was willing to give. When he left for school, he'd still had a mother. When he left for school, his mother, still in her bathrobe, had run after him as far as the garden gate. As always, even when it wasn't yet above fifty degrees, or already under fifty. Meanwhile he's almost twice as tall as when he first started school, but that doesn't stop her from running after him as far as the garden gate holding his cap: *Put your hat on, sweetheart*. It didn't stop her from running after him until today. Beyond where the street curves, his mother couldn't see him any longer, and he would take the cap off again. He never felt cold, but his mother didn't believe him. The housekeeper says she wants to go home now, she's in a state from all that's happened, but if he needs help, tomorrow or whenever, he knows where to find her. To go home now. He nods and pulls the door shut behind her.

How is he ever supposed to go up these steps again? The carpeting covering the steps is scraped in one spot, is that the spot? Or were those scratches always there? Did his mother slip or stumble? On which of these steps was her head lying when she stopped breathing? But even if he knew everything about the final moments of his mother's life, he still wouldn't know what it meant now for her to be dead. *Yesterday the great artist H., recipient of the Comrade G. Medal, the Badge of Honor of the Great Patriotic Order of Merit in Gold, and the Goethe Prize, as well as a number of other highly prestigious awards bestowed by our Republic, was suddenly and unexpectedly taken from us. We shall eternally hold our stalwart Comrade H., the courageous antifascist faithfully devoted to the workers' cause, in reverent memory.*

8

She falls and, falling, asks herself whether this fall is really going to end with her breaking her neck.

You know, I never heard back from them about the streetcar stop on Kastanienallee at the corner of Schönhauser.

Be patient, they'll get back to you, her husband says, brushing the strand of hair back from his face.

If they'd just move the streetcar stop forward a little, there wouldn't be a traffic jam there day after day.

She falls, and while she is falling she feels ashamed for falling.

Come on, that could happen to anyone.

I also wrote to them about conditions at the Landsberg retirement home. They need to hire more staff, the old people there are really suffering, someone told me.

That was the right thing to do.

And about the Intourist trips to Finland—they're so disorganized!

Is Finland pretty?

Of course. And just imagine, you can't order any replacement parts direct from the factory that makes all the carburetors and filters for our Republic.

Really!

That's got to change.

Most definitely.

She is tumbling out of this world in which so much remains to be done before everything is as it should be. When she isn't here any longer, who will care for this State that is her State and still in short trousers?

9

Stepping over the invisible body of his mother—or rather, through it—he now ascends the stairs after all, to the upper floor. Starting now, every time he goes up the stairs, he will be walking over his mother's invisible body, or through it. Actually all his mother did was switch sides. But he doesn't know where the sides are. Time and eternity: there's no just stepping into eternity. You can only get there by falling. And how do you fall?

The bathrobe his mother was still wearing when she said good-bye to him at the garden gate is now hanging in the bathroom. On the hook she always hangs it on when she gets dressed. Always hung it on when she got dressed. Without knowing why, he puts his hand into the pocket of the bathrobe and finds a used tissue. This tissue still exists in the present out of which his mother has fallen. *If I catch you one more time climbing around in the ruins!* Without him, she would be all alone in the world! Now it's the other way around. He goes down the stairs again, through his invisible mother.

There was scarcely any other author who succeeded in portraying our Socialist reconstruction as vividly as our great writer H., whose life came to a tragic end so abruptly and unexpectedly the day before last.

Actually everything's just as it was before. In the parlor, the bouquet on the table is still perfectly fresh. He sits down on the sofa on which the Minister of Culture has sat many times before, and the daughter of the President, a good friend of his mother's; and the head of the so-called "Salad Brigade" at the fish-processing facility at Sassnitz has sat here too (the Salad Brigade that was named in his mother's honor), as has one of the first great activists, Adolf Hennecke, who lives only two houses down; eight-year-old pioneers sat here on this sofa in front of his famous mother and wanted to know how one becomes a writer; a woman sick with rheumatism sat down exactly where he is sitting now to ask whether his mother could possibly write a letter asking for her to be allowed to go to the health resort in Sochi; the head of the Writers' Union sat here as well, and on another occasion the artistic director of the theater Volksbühne Berlin, along with the famous actor who played the lead in his mother's famous play, and from time to time the famous sculptor sat here too, who received the Patriotic Order of Merit at the same time she did, and just recently the famous composer sat here, who wants to write an opera based on a text by her.

Now he, her seventeen-year-old son, is sitting on this sofa in front of the bouquet that has not yet even begun to wilt, gazing at his invisible mother, who sits in the armchair she always sat in when visitors came.

And my father?

He fell in the battle of Kharkov.

As darkness gradually falls, he tries to imagine the enormous quantity of time he will now spend without his mother. Along with her life, the memories he might have of her have stopped growing as well. Be grateful for what you've got, his mother always said. But sooner or later, because of his forgetfulness, he will lose his mother all over again—this time piecemeal.

The big window that leads from the parlor out to the terrace is now entirely dark.

On many evenings of many years, from spring into fall, he had sat with his mother on this terrace. Here she told him of Valentinovka, where they used to spend their Moscow summers: she, his father, who fell at the battle of Kharkov, and her friend O. The leaves here smell exactly like the leaves there, she'd always said. Only in Valentinovka there was a little river across the way where she used to go swimming every morning before breakfast. No doubt because of these stories his mother liked to tell, he always imagines trees when someone speaks of Moscow, and yellow leaves that have come to rest on a damp meadow, he sees not the Kremlin and its golden towers but a small, sun-dappled river, sees weeds beneath the surface being swept gently back and forth by the current, and minnows.

Was his mother so afraid of storms back then? For as long as he's known her, she's been terrified not only of thunder and lightning but also of wind that might suddenly gust through the house, smashing everything to pieces. *Did you close the terrace door tightly?* Yes. *And the dining room window?* Yes. *Then I'll go upstairs.* Okay. *The terrace door?* I said yes. Then she would go upstairs to her bedroom,

185

closing the door there carefully as well, and she wouldn't come out again until all that remained of the storm was the rain.

But on warm evenings he and his mother would often sit until nightfall on the terrace. She would read, and he would do his homework or write the monthly report for his *Free German Youth* class group.

Can you help me?

What sort of outing was it?

We went to the Pergamon Museum.

So write: We went to the Pergamon Museum.

That's not enough.

Oh, I see. So write that you investigated the history of the class struggle by studying the ancient society of slave holders.

That's good.

Did you notice how tall the steps are that lead up to the Pergamon Altar?

Yes.

That's how they build things when people are supposed to be in awe of their own gods.

Should I write that?

No.

His mother was sitting outside, close to the light, and he ducked into the house for a minute to fetch something, a glass of water, a pad of paper, a ruler. As he returned, he saw her from behind from deep in the interior of the dark house. His mother had a book on her knees, but she wasn't reading, she just sat there gazing out into the night. She didn't turn around to look at him. After all, she knew he was on his way back. She had a thick jacket on since it was already quite chilly.

Why did you call me just plain Sasha and not Alexander?

Why didn't you ever go up to the attic?

What are the best apples to use for strudel?

186

Along with his mother, the answers to all these questions have died as well.

Was there still snow on the ground that April in Ufa when I was born?

Was the first word I spoke German or Russian?

What was the name of my *niania*?

Along with his mother, the way she looked at him died, and everything beyond what he himself remembers. He will now never be old enough to learn the things she hadn't yet told him, even if he lives to be eighty.

Do you really not have a photograph of my father?

His invisible mother sits with her back to him in silence, giving no answer.

10

Was her son even listening when she told him about all the new things they were trying to do here?

In the sunlit silence of a Sabbath, a letter falls from an opening hand into a hand that someone is holding out.

Why is she only now remembering what her grandmother told her half a lifetime ago?

But then one of them must be intending to deliver the letter and the other to receive it, she had replied to her grandmother.

That's right.

And having these intentions is not work?

If only she could remember her grandmother's reply to this question, all would be well again.

But she can't remember.

She falls.

11

Often he'd been afraid that he would lose her. Sometimes she would have fainting fits, just keeling over suddenly, breathing with such difficulty that he thought she might suffocate. At moments like this, she would look different, too, not like his mother at all. Surviving, that meant for him above all that she was turning back into the mother he knew.

Could he himself have been responsible for what she called her "fits"?

As a child he had sometimes forgotten how easily she could get worked up. Once, for example, he took her linen-cupboard key from its secret hook because he needed a pillowcase for a carnival costume. How dare he go through her linens without asking permission? Or when he and his friends exploded homemade fireworks in the garden. Or jumped off the roof of the terrace with an umbrella to learn how to fly. Or once he had hidden in a crate up in the attic and waited to see if his mother would find him—though he knew even then that she never went up to the attic. When at last he came out of hiding, there were two *Volkspolizei* officers standing in the hall, and his mother was sitting in tears on the lowest step of the stairs.

The stairs.

And three years ago the *major incident*, as his mother always calls it. Always called it. His first girlfriend was just visiting him when his mother returned home from a trip. He hadn't heard the doorbell. His mother suddenly came into his room without knocking, and after one look at the young couple kissing, she'd slammed the door shut again. He had gotten his girlfriend out of the house as quickly as he could, and she never again came to see him, but nevertheless this *major incident* was perhaps related to his mother's first heart attack. Only a few weeks later she collapsed in her study and was taken away with sirens howling.

★

Whenever his mother was at the hospital being examined, or off at a resort, or on a journey, he had taken to just staying home with the housekeeper, who would cook for him after school and then leave. The housekeeper smelled of perspiration. When he was younger, his mother had hired this or that nanny to live with him in the house while she was on the road—because she had readings or premieres of her plays in other cities, or was traveling to Poland with Writers Union delegations, or to Czechoslovakia or Hungary. One of the nannies used to spray saliva when she read to him, another pinched his cheek when she said hello, the third refused to return to his bedside out of principle when he was afraid of the dark and cried out for her.

This housekeeper smelled of perspiration.

At least he doesn't have to worry about his mother any longer.

It's quite certain now that she will never again turn back into the mother he knows.

And his father?

He fell in the battle of Kharkov.

12

As if one final moment existed within another, simultaneously present, she can remember exactly what that morning was like when she said goodbye to her grandmother. One day before she traveled to Prague under a false name. The miniature grandfather clock was just striking eleven with tinny strokes; her grandmother wrapped a pair of challahs in a cloth for her and gave her a slip of paper on which she'd written the recipe. The skin on her grandmother's hands was so thin the veins showed through, violet.

But time has blurred all those things that happened for the last time without it being called the last time. At some point her mother had pinned up her hair for her for the last time. At some point she herself had washed the dishes for the last time while her sister sat at the kitchen table doing her homework. At some point she sat in Krasni Mak for the last time. At many points during her life she had done something for the last time without knowing it. Did that mean that death was not a moment but a front, one that was as long as life? And so was she tumbling not only out of this world, but out of all possible worlds? Was she tumbling out of Vienna, out of Prague and Moscow, out of Berlin, out of the Socialist sister countries and the western world? Tumbling out of the entire world, out of all the time there ever was, would be, is? But now what will happen to her son?

13

At the funeral, the urn containing his mother's ashes sits on a pedestal up front between two flags. The red flag on the left is draped as if it were blowing to the left, and the national flag on the right as if it were blowing to the right. Whose idea was it to drape the flags to look as if a storm were rising from the urn? Ridiculous, his mother would have said.

His mother had just recently been to the hairdresser's to have her color touched up. Now her freshly coiffed hair has been incinerated, and her face is also ash, her shoulders, too, are there in this bronze-colored canister, and her hands as well with their fleshy fingertips, her round knees, her feet, and even her toes, painted mother-of-pearl. He's never seen his mother naked, but he's seen how she looks when she is asleep, or how she crosses one leg over the other when she is sitting, he's seen how she waits, how she pours herself a glass of water, how she gets up, puts on a coat, how she reaches for her handbag, how she walks. The body of his mother was the landscape he knew best among all the landscapes in the world.

14

In front of her, an ancient woman is shaking what looks like a child's rattle made of ivory, with silver bells. She stops. Shakes. Stops. When the bells have rung for the third time, she goes into the theater.

15

In the middle, leaning up against the pedestal with the urn, is his wreath with the ribbon printed in black script: *For my mother*. In front of it: the wreath sent by the Central Committee of the Party: *Our estimable comrade*; the wreath from the Council of Ministers: *Stalwart in the struggle*; the wreath from the People's Parliament: *With Socialist salutations*; the wreath from the Magistrate of Berlin, the capital of the GDR: *To an honorary citizen of our city*; the wreath sent by the Writers Union: *To a great writer*; and: *Unforgotten*, the wreath of the Cultural Association of the GDR.

Who arranged the ribbons in such a way that you can read all the farewells?

A fortnight ago it was still a fortnight before he would be sitting here in front of her urn, but he hadn't known it yet.

Just to the right of the urn is a little stand with a velvet cushion on which his mother's medals are displayed: The Comrade G. Medal, the Patriotic Order of Merit, the Goethe Prize, and, twice, the Workers' Pennant.

Ten days ago it was ten days before.

And just to the right of the urn, a table with her books.

The music they are playing is by Beethoven, according to the program. Who picked the music?

So did time keep rushing ever more rapidly away until it was gone? Why hadn't he noticed? Why hadn't his mother?

16

It is she herself who slices through the paper, splitting the entire stack from top to bottom at one go.

17

The Minister of Culture gives the first speech.

In Ufa his wife gave me the first two diapers for you.

Then there's music again, this time the dirge: *Victims immortal, you sank into dust. We stand here and mourn as our hearts say we must.*

I like the lyrics better in Russian.

Then the second speech, given by the President of the Academy of Arts.

He's one of those functionaries who write on the side.

One week ago today, his mother was still alive. The lees of her life were already slipping away, but she had moved around just as deliberately as ever. He had never once, for example, seen his mother running. From a distance, she had always looked like an old woman, bent over and somehow crooked, even when she was just fifty.

18

What are all these people waiting in line for? Are they giving away darkness for free? But that won't curb anyone's hunger.

19

At the end they play a piece by Haydn, during which everyone stands up, and her son goes to the front of the room in order to carry his wreath himself, as arranged with the funeral director. The urn, the velvet cushion with his mother's medals, the books, the flags, and the official wreaths are picked up by soldiers of the Guards Regiment and carried, at the head of the funeral procession, to the gravesite. The son, in his role as first mourner, walks right behind the soldier carrying the urn, but because the urn-bearer is leading the procession so slowly, he has to pay attention not to step on the man's heels. Is the Guards Regiment trying to compel the guests to assume a mournful state with this slow pace? Is the Guards Regiment standing guard over the mourners' sentiments to ensure that the officially prescribed levels of grief are maintained?

20

From the darkness a small hand reaches out to her, something yellow in its palm. Ah, finally Sasha is handing her the lemon she's been waiting for all this time.

21

When they reach the grave, the flag bearers dip their two flags while the urn is lowered into the pit. *Forward, brothers and sisters, and the Last Judgment let us face.* Oops, must have misheard—he knows perfectly well that the trumpets of the working class call the brothers and sisters to the last fight, not the Last Judgment. But isn't the last fight death? *The Internationa-a-le. Unites. The hu. Man race.*

The son now takes up position, as arranged, to the left of the grave, behind him the table with his mother's books. On the other side of the grave, the velvet cushion with the medals has been set on a pedestal again, and between the medals and the grave stands a cemetery worker offering the mourners rose petals from five baskets.

Anyone who joins this line must first pass by the cushion with his mother's medals, then the cemetery worker, then the grave with the little bronze-colored pot at the bottom, finally arriving before him, the only son of the deceased.

The son shakes hands.

He shakes the hand of the President's daughter and the hand of the President himself, shakes the hand of the artistic director of the Volksbühne Berlin, shakes many hands of famous writers, famous sculptors, and famous composers, he shakes the hand of the woman with rheumatism, the hand of the Deputy Ambassador of the Soviet Union in Berlin, Capital of the GDR, and also the hand of the brigade leader of the Salad Division of the fish-processing plant Sassnitz; he shakes the small hands of pioneers, the young hands of women who perhaps want to be writers themselves some day, and the old hands of comrades who knew his mother from Moscow, Prague, or Ufa.

At the very end of the reception line, he holds out his hand to a man he doesn't know, and this man looks at him with his own gray-blue eyes, the mouth of the man looks exactly like his own mouth that he sees every morning in the mirror. With exactly the same sort of raspy voice he himself has, the man, after clearing his throat, utters his heartfelt condolences, except that his heartfelt condolences sound different from those of the others—they're called *soboleznovaniya*—reminding the son so abruptly of his own Russian childhood, it's as if his memory were a curtain suddenly ripping in two.

22

Thank you, he says, and the man nods to him, but then others arrive wanting to shake the son's hand, and by the time the line is finally at an end and the funeral director places his mother's medals back in their proper boxes, handing them to him, and a soldier of the Guards Regiment places his mother's books in a bag, carrying them away, and a gravedigger begins to fill up the pit again with pale Brandenburg sand, and one or another of his mother's friends, their eyes filled with tears, strokes the son's head one last time as they are leaving, by the time the group of mourners has finally dispersed and departed, the stranger is nowhere to be seen, and he, the sole survivor, the son of the deceased who has not yet even reached the age of maturity, takes streetcar No. 46 back to the house where he has lived until now together with his mother, and where there is now no one awaiting him.

Please take off your shoes in the hall. Walking through his invisible mother, he climbs the stairs, goes into his mother's dressing room, takes the key from its secret hook, and unlocks the linen cabinet. Inside are duvet covers, pillowcases, towels, and sheets.

At the very bottom, under the sheets, is a sealed letter.

Russian stamps, a Vienna address in his mother's handwriting, and above it a stamped message adorned with a swastika: *Evacuated to the East*.

At some point his mother slid this letter under the sheets.

Now he has retrieved it.

He looks at the envelope, turns it over, and on the back is an address in Cyrillic script.

He slides the letter back under the sheets.

But now the hiding place is no longer a hiding place.

Does she really not have a photograph of his father?

On the evening of this day he takes out the atlas from his mother's bookshelf.

Where is Kharkov anyhow?

23

The next morning is Sunday.

The next morning his mother is still dead.

If only she would stop being dead soon, he thinks.

If only the stairs didn't exist, his mother would still be alive, he thinks.

If only they hadn't moved into this house with a staircase.

If only his mother hadn't liked this house so much.

If only she hadn't liked this place so much where she would break her neck.

Those stairs are treacherous.

In his mother's atlas, still lying open on his table from the night before, he flips from the Ukrainian Soviet Republic, featuring the major city Kharkov, back to the page that shows Berlin. Scientific convention has assigned Berlin, this city where his mother was until recently still alive and where she is now dead, the coordinates 52.58373 degrees latitude north and 13.39667 degrees longitude east (coordinates that were assigned to this place before her death and remain assigned to it now). And since, after all, human beings can't go strolling around on the moon and falling down dead there, it stands to reason that two of the coordinates in his atlas must be the coordinates of the place where he himself will stop living. Where his bones will rot. A place he doesn't know yet—and by the time he does, it won't do him any good.

Mama, does that mean that some day my body will be my corpse?

With all its birthmarks and scars, with the skin, hair, and veins I know so well already? Does that mean I'm basically sharing my entire life with my corpse? Is that how it is, Mama? You grow up, you get old, and when the corpse is ready, it's time to die?

Since his mother is no longer winding the clock on the wall, it's quieter in the house than ever.

So now in this world that has been surveyed to within an inch of its life, he is alone.

Alone.

Alone with shelves filled with books, cabinets containing drawers filled with files and notes; alone with chairs, beds, tables, sofas, cupboards, coat hooks and lamps; alone with the chandelier, with rugs, a rattan trunk, winter coats, with his mother's typewriter; alone with bottle openers, aspirin, bed linens, scouring powder, tools, shoes, and pots, with ironing board, laundry rack, tea table, and the wall hanging with the huge yellow sun, with broom and mop, his mother's combs, brushes, and makeup, with shower gel and skin creams, dishes, knives, and forks, flower vases, paper clips, envelopes, his mother's diaries and manuscripts, records and a record player, eight bottles of wine, a music box, chains, rings, and brooches, two cans of lentils, a refrigerator containing half a stick of butter, three tubs of yogurt, two slices of cheese; he's alone with a revolving chair, countless drawings and lithographs in varying formats, several paintings, one of them a portrait of his mother; alone with ten apples, a loaf of bread, with sundry pencils, pens, erasers, and stacks of white paper; alone with twine, coasters, potholders, with coins and bills from many lands, with mirrors, extension cords, and a tabletop fountain that no longer works; alone with two potted rubber trees, several coverlets, woolen blankets, pillows, with empty suitcases, handbags, house slippers, nutcrackers, tablecloths and carbon paper, towels, eyeglasses, sweaters, stockings and blouses, underwear; alone with his mother's cardigans and scarves; alone with his own first sweater and cap from when he himself was still an infant, and a little cutting board he painted back in kindergarten in Moscow.

Alone.

Will he have to pick up her glasses to remember her eyes, her wallet to remember her fingers, a pair of shoes to see her feet eternally in their shoes, and her woolen blanket to remember until the end of days how her body looked when she was napping after lunch? How many objects and coverings will be needed if she is to retain at least a life of memory inside him? But probably there isn't anything his mother's hands, reaching out from the realm of the dead, will be able to grasp so firmly—no object, no piece of furniture, or item of clothing—as she grasps him, the one to whom she first bequeathed her heartbeat, and then, when he was still small, whose diapers she changed and whose nose she wiped, whom she looked at again and again, watching and observing him, and whom later, as he grew, she taught language and read to, whose hand she held to cross larger streets, whose hair she combed, whose sweater she pulled on over his head and whose shoes she tied, whom she looked at again and again, watching and observing him, whom she consoled when he fell down, whose temperature she took and whom she taught to ride a bicycle, to whom she said what she found good and proper and what wrong, what she found tedious, amusing, interesting, whom she looked at again and again, watching and observing him, whom she scolded, shouted at and cursed, and often also praised and kissed. For the first time now, he tries to see himself through his mother's eyes, from the outside, as it were, but this is difficult. Strange, he thinks, that we use *blind spot* to designate a place that cannot clearly be seen because it is too close. Still, memory no doubt prefers to be able to exchange the bit of blindness for a living body.

During spring break he'll start cleaning out the house, and in the summer he's supposed to move to a Home where he'll spend the final year before he comes of age, his legal guardian told him.

When the doorbell rings, he knows that on a Sunday it can be neither the mailman nor the housekeeper.

The man looks at him with his own gray-blue eyes, and the mouth of the man looks exactly like his own mouth that he sees every morning in the mirror. With exactly the same sort of raspy voice he himself has, the man, after clearing his throat, says *good day* in Russian.

In the pause that follows, German silence and Russian silence intermingle.

And then the boy's father grabs him by his shock of hair and pulls him in for a hug.

Like an exhausted boxer, the boy remains briefly in his embrace before pushing away.

From the hall you can see into his mother's study.

Is that where she wrote? his father asks.

Yes.

Would you make us some tea?

The boy nods.

While the boy puts on the kettle, takes out cups and tea from the cupboard, and finally pours the water, his father leans against the doorpost, watching his son move around busily, picking things up and putting them down.

When the tea is ready, the boy's father picks up the teapot and leads the way.

Let's sit in here, his father says, walking into his mother's study.

This is the first time for as long as the boy can remember that a visitor is taking a seat not in the parlor but at the little tea table in his mother's study. On the wall is the wall hanging with the huge yellow sun.

Do you really live in Kharkov?

Why Kharkov?

The boy shrugs. He sits bent over in his chair, the cup in his hands.

At first the father hears only a regular dripping sound, then he sees the rings forming in his son's teacup, a new ring each time a tear falls from the tip of the boy's nose into the tea.

When I met your mother, she was going through some difficult times.

Everything started when I asked whether her husband had returned home yet and she burst into tears.

I wanted to give her my handkerchief, but there was still a knot in it.

The knot was so tight that I couldn't get it open right away.

That was how it started. . . .

Maybe you need one yourself?

Yes, please.

The father pulls a pressed handkerchief out of his front pocket and gives it to his son.

What was the knot supposed to remind you of?

That there was an assembly that night.

And then?

I forgot the assembly.

INTERMEZZO

If she'd gone downstairs just five minutes later, she'd have missed the entrance to the underworld, which would have trundled on its way, offering its open hole to someone else instead; or if she'd taken that step with her right foot instead of her left, she wouldn't have lost her footing; or if she'd been thinking not about this and that but about that and this, she'd have seen the steps instead of not seeing them. Even so, some death or other will eventually be her death. If not sooner, then later. Some entrance will have to be for her. Every last person, every he and every she, has an entrance meant for him, for her. So does this underworld consist only of holes? Is there nothing more to it? A different wind is blowing here. Is there nothing that could prevent a person from—sooner or later, here or there—stumbling right into it, flailing, falling, plummeting, sinking?

In the fall of '89, the partition between the Eastern and Western parts of Germany collapses: it gets flattened, breached and scorned, and the mob that's been working itself into a frenzy stampedes out of its own country and flings itself into the arms of its capitalist brothers and sisters—joy, rapture and sweet oblivion—an entire body politic is emptied out, thrown up (why is it throwing when you throw up), surrendering all power, all sovereignty, then collapsing, spent. Now another wind is blowing, something that used to be called a life is now called forty years of waiting that have only now proved worthwhile. What's a five-year plan? Everything is being called by different names, new "shores" on the horizon. Words, which long ago stopped being as real as a bag of flour or a pair of shoes, have failed, becoming economically unsustainable. Twenty sorts of butter, whereas before there was just one, rents are now being multiplied by ten, different plays are being put on at the theater, the Russians are closing their barracks and selling their forefathers' fur hats, uniform jackets, and medals from the Great Patriotic War at the *Strasse des 17. Juni* flea market. On June 17, 1953, workers in East Berlin staged a revolt against the excessive quotas being imposed on them, but they were unsuccessful, while the miner and early activist Adolf Hennecke (pioneer of the quota) was now living in a villa in Pankow. Down with privileges! In 1990, former government ministers, currently unemployed, lean on their garden fences, chatting with retirees out walking their dogs. Whether they will be allowed to hold on to these properties is being looked into. The Easterners head to the West to collect their welcome payments, and return home Westerners. East is no longer anything more than a point on the compass. The publishing house that printed the books of the *estimable author* goes bankrupt. The readers have other things to do than read these days, first they want a trip to the Canaries. *It is not enough to be eighteen years old.* The century that used to be so young is now terribly old. His mother, too, is old.

Her son comes to visit her on Sunday at four.

She says she's realized that she's been hiding things and she no longer remembers where. She says she's no longer herself.

The housekeeper brings coffee and cake on a tray, then she goes back out again.

Mother to son: Should I kill myself?

Her son says: Of course not, Mother.

He says: Oh, Mother.

He says: How can you ask such a thing?

The son visits his mother on Sunday at four, his mother has a forearm that is completely black and blue. He asks: Did you fall?

No, his mother says. She says that her skin just turns black and blue like that in certain spots all by itself.

In the kitchen, the housekeeper tells the son that she doesn't think that's true, but his mother never tells her anything.

The son comes to visit his mother on Sunday at four. As the housekeeper is taking his coat, she says that his mother has only been awake for half an hour since when she arrived in the morning to start work, she'd found his mother sitting fully dressed on the edge of the bed, where she'd apparently been since the evening before. So she put her to bed for the day.

Thank you, the son says. Thank you so much for all your trouble.

Then the housekeeper calls the son at 7:30 in the morning, saying his mother is not at home. Is she with him? The son says: No. He says: I'll be right over.

The son cancels a meeting, tells his older child that he'll have to take the bus to school and that he should get a move on since it is already late, asks his wife to take their younger child to school, and his wife says: Are you out of your mind? I've got make-up at 8:30, oh right, the father says, and calls his daughter's school to say she's ill, when he hangs up, his daughter says: It's bad to tell lies, and her father says: Get a book, read, and wait until I get home.

Then the son drives to his mother's house.

The housekeeper says: What am I supposed to do?

The son: It's not your fault.

The son goes searching for his mother in all the surrounding streets. Somewhere or other, she is sitting on the curb in her nightshirt, crying.

That night, when the children are in bed, the son says to his wife: Things can't go on like this with my mother.

His wife says: I don't know what you mean.

My mother owns a large house.

His wife says: Forget it.

The man says: I know it wouldn't be easy for you.

The woman: She kept trying to turn the children against me. If you're in the mood for a war, sure, let's go move in with her.

The man: But she can't look after herself anymore.

She didn't help me with the children even once that entire year you were in Leningrad.

It's just that she can't take it when the boy plays his music so loud.

And the girl?

It was just too much responsibility for her.

You see, now I'm the one who can't take it, and it's just too much responsibility for me.

We're all going to be old some day.

I'll be damned if I'll go blackmailing my children when the time comes.

She's not blackmailing me.

Oh, really?

She doesn't know what she's doing any longer.

Serves her right for playing the know-it-all for so many years.

What an ugly thing to say.

Now she's even going to drive us apart.

Nonsense.

BOOK V

1

The week Frau Hoffmann is going to die, the day after her nine-tieth birthday, Sister Renate has the early shift.

The week Frau Hoffmann is going to die, the day after her nine-tieth birthday, she is sharing a room—just as she's done for seven months now—with Frau Buschwitz, whose habit it is to scratch and slap anyone who comes within three feet of her. The day Frau Buschwitz moved into Frau Hoffmann's room, Frau Hoffmann fought her first and only battle with her new roommate, she'd ap-proached Frau Buschwitz intending a friendly greeting, whereupon Frau Buschwitz took a swipe at her, as was her wont, prompting Frau Hoffmann in her surprise to hunt for the nearest object within reach that she might use to defend herself, and what she found was a piece of zwieback lying on the table. She scraped this zwieback right across Frau Buschwitz's face, whereupon Frau Buschwitz re-treated. From then on, Frau Hoffmann has never gone within three feet of her roommate.

This week, too—the week she is going to die, the day after her ninetieth birthday—begins with a Monday, just like every other week, and this Monday, too, begins with breakfast at eight, just like every other day. Breakfast begins, as always, with the attendant on duty pushing her in her wheelchair from her room to the breakfast room, giving Frau Buschwitz a wide berth.

What is a Monday? Frau Hoffmann sits at the long table, as always, between Frau Schröder and Frau Millner, who are still able to sit in chairs. Between the chairs of Frau Schröder and Frau Millner, a place, as always, has been left empty for her wheelchair. Frau Hoffmann's red hair is now gray as well, such that a person who knew her before would have a hard time picking her out from among all the many nodding, tilted, dozing, or bent gray- and white-haired heads. When Frau Hoffmann speaks at breakfast, it disturbs no one here, for the ears of all these ladies and gentlemen are really quite old. And if jam falls on her blouse, it disturbs no one, for the eyes of all these ladies and gentlemen are old as well. After a few bites she pushes her breakfast plate away and refuses to eat anything more.

Thousands have been invited here for this meal, from many different levels. But this I cannot eat.

Sister Renate, who is pouring tea, says:

But Frau Hoffmann, there really aren't thousands of us here.

Yes—thousands! And I don't know why these people have assembled here, I cannot determine the cause, the purpose of this meeting—but it must have a purpose!

Frau Hoffmann, please eat your breakfast.

It's so paltry! There ought to be more selection. Why are all these thousands eating this mess that is served here?

Fresh rolls straight from the bakery, Frau Hoffmann.

There'll have to be a discussion of this some time, this food and the purpose of everyone having only this paltry mess to eat—but I haven't yet been able to speak with anyone about this.

But, but, Frau Hoffmann.

I can't eat it. First I must determine what sort of development—developments of all different sorts!—these individuals have gone through, what motivates them, what might win them over, and what not.

Between 8:30 and 9:30, after the breakfast has been cleared away, it isn't worth having yourself wheeled back into your room. You sit where you are. At 9:30 everyone in wheelchairs goes to the exercise room, where the fingers, hands, feet and heads of those who can no longer get up, or at least not on their own, are worked over, and at 11:00 it's back to the day room. From 11:00 until 11:30 everyone sits there. The TV is on. On the wall is a large clock. Some are asleep in their wheelchairs, wrapped up in blankets.

She would like to read. If she held the book close to her eyes, she would even be able to decipher the letters, but her arms and hands aren't strong enough to hold the book.

Frau Zeisig was an excellent skier.

Down we go! I so wish I could go whizzing down the slope just once more, but it's not possible.

Herr Behrendt was a pastor.

I so wish I could write something down sometimes, but my head won't cooperate.

Frau Braun walked all the way from Heydekrug on the Memel to Berlin after the war, with three children.

No one can quite imagine what that means anymore.

And all of them survived.

All three of them proper, lovely children.

From the kitchen, the clinking of plates can be heard.

My oldest recently celebrated his own golden anniversary.

It smells of stew. The staff sets the table. The day room is full of desires. At 11:30 lunch is served.

Frau Hoffmann says to Frau Millner, who is hard of hearing:

We have to organize our group. A few of them will show up early, others late—we have to coordinate all of that and then await orders from leadership.

Frau Millner doesn't look at Frau Hoffmann, she is trying to spear the little shreds of chicken in her fricassee on her fork.

We cannot under any circumstances take action until the orders have reached us.

Frau Millner nods, but not because she agrees with Frau Hoffmann; she nods because the fricassee tastes good.

I've been waiting for my husband, Frau Hoffmann says. I always stood there on the corner, waiting. I've spent my whole life standing on the corner, waiting.

Frau Hoffmann, Sister Renate says in passing, you've got to eat something, too.

If I start eating, Frau Hoffmann says, it'll make me feel awful.

But, but, says Sister Renate.

I can't.

Just one spoonful at least, Frau Hoffmann.

It would be good if I could eat something, that would make life more stable somehow.

Precisely, Frau Hoffmann.

But I can't.

After lunch she tries pushing the wheels of her wheelchair herself to return to her room, but she doesn't get anywhere because she doesn't have the strength in her hands.

Oh, Frau Hoffmann, let me give you a hand, Sister Renate says, helping her.

On the way to her room, Frau Hoffmann looks down the corridor and at its end she sees the young attendant coming out of one of the many doors, she calls: Hey there, hey! And lifts one hand to wave, but he appears to be in a hurry or perhaps he didn't hear her shout, already he's vanished behind one of the many other doors.

He doesn't have time for you right now, Frau Hoffmann, maybe later.

Frau Hoffmann nods. We've got to be a little bit patient, don't we?

Precisely, Frau Hoffmann.

For our struggle.

Of course.

But that's not such an easy thing to do.

No, you're certainly right.

The nurse pushes the wheelchair into the room, giving a wide berth to the bed of Frau Buschwitz, who has lain down for an after-lunch nap.

Next to the window, Frau Hoffmann?

Yes, please.

When the nurse has locked the wheels and is about to leave, Frau Hoffmann grabs her by the sleeve:

What should I do now?

That's not something I can tell you, Frau Hoffmann, the nurse says and brushes the elderly hand from her sleeve—the hand is cold—lays Frau Hoffmann's cold hand back in her lap and leaves. The doors in this place shut so softly, Frau Hoffmann doesn't hear that the nurse is already gone.

Why and what? she inquires of the early afternoon silence, but receives no answer.

Her body is a city. Her heart is a large shady square, her fingers pedestrians, her hair the light of streetlamps, her knees two rows of buildings. She tries to give people footpaths. She tries to open up her cheeks and her towers. She didn't know streets hurt so much, nor that there were so many streets in her to begin with. She wants to take her body on a stroll, out of her body, but she doesn't know where the key is. I'm afraid of losing my head. Afraid someone might take the key of my head away from me.

At 3 p.m. there's coffee along with a little bowl of ice cream. Frau Buschwitz had someone wheel her out of the room, but Frau Hoffmann stays where she is, drinking the coffee and stirring the ice cream around until it melts, then she slurps it up spoonful by spoonful. There's a knock at the door. It's Herr Zabel from Residential

Area III, who sometimes stops by for a visit when he can't find his wife, she died twelve years ago.

Frau Hoffmann, do you happen to know where my wife is?

What does she look like?

She has curly brown hair down to her shoulders and likes to laugh.

No, she hasn't been here, but if she shows up, I'll tell her you're looking for her.

That's very kind of you, Frau Hoffmann.

Herr Zabel has forgotten many times now that his wife is dead, and so again and again the horrific news of her death comes crashing down on him with all its weight whenever someone who hasn't been paying attention replies:

Your wife? But she's been dead for years!

He's had to mourn his wife's loss all over again many times now, but Frau Hoffmann—and for this she has his eternal gratitude—always promises to let him know if his wife passes by. Herr Zabel also enjoys sitting down to chat with Frau Hoffmann for a little while. She is courteous, and he can speak with her about anything that troubles him. He might say, for example:

I am slowly but sickly beginning to be an animal.

And Frau Hoffmann says:

I'm afraid of gradually becoming transparent in both directions.

And Herr Zabel says:

The sick are beginning to abandon their honor.

And Frau Hoffmann says:

It is so difficult to bear all of this.

And Herr Zabel:

Why don't we try biting open our illnesses?

This reminds Frau Hoffmann of a verse from her childhood:

God our Father whom we love, you gave us teeth, now give us food.

And Herr Zabel adds:

God our Father whom we love, if we're all one, make us all good.

Strange, isn't it, Frau Hoffmann says, the way one word can find its way through the thicket of all the words.

Yes, it certainly is strange, Herr Zabel says, and he remains silent for a while.

At some point he gets up, makes a little bow in Frau Hoffmann's direction and goes back to his room in Residential Area III; after all, his wife might be on her way there herself by now.

At 5:30, all those who are able to walk or can be pushed in wheelchairs are summoned to the dining room. At six, dinner is served. Frau Hoffmann still uses the Viennese word *Nachtmahl* or "night meal," even though it's been a lifetime since she lived there. The space for her wheelchair is between Frau Schröder and Frau Millner.

What a fuss people make about eating, Frau Hoffmann says to Sister Katrin, who is cutting an open-face sandwich into little squares for her.

People go out for *fine dining*, she says with a little bleat of laughter.

It's nice to go out, Sister Katrin says, candlelight dinners, don't you agree, Frau Hoffmann?

And really you're only eating so you won't die.

Goodness, Frau Hoffmann. Bon appétit!

Without eating, you die, that's all there is to it, Frau Hoffmann says.

But Sister Katrin isn't listening any longer, she's moved on to one of the other tables, where she's busy tying a bib around a woman's neck.

It's just because you *have* to eat that people make such a fuss about it, Frau Hoffmann says.

But neither Frau Schröder nor Frau Millner can hear what her neighbor is saying.

It's just to keep people from getting bored, she says.

215

Then the evening comes.

Frau Buschwitz has put on her headphones and begun to listen to the radio. Sister Katrin helped Frau Hoffmann change into her nightgown and held the drinking glass for her while she sat on the edge of her bed and swallowed her pills. Then Sister Katrin left.

Frau Hoffman can see quite clearly that someone has meanwhile taken a seat in her armchair next to the window. And although it's been a long time since she last saw her, she recognizes this visitor at once. Against the yellow evening sky she looks like a silhouette.

I find myself in a transitional stage, Frau Hoffmann says.

Her mother is silent.

And I don't know what to do, Frau Hoffmann says.

Her mother is silent.

The question is whether I'll be able to hold out against him. He's very powerful, and he's very cruel to me. I'd have asked for a bit more kindness. But he doesn't know anything about kindness. He's rough with me, and cruel.

Her mother is silent.

It's going to be a goddamn fight. I'm not the one attacking. It's him attacking me—him or her. He or she is attacking me, from all sides. But I don't want—I still have so many, so many possibilities. There are many things I don't remember, but still something . . .

Oh, *meydele*, her mother says all at once, and her voice doesn't really sound old.

I would like to take steps against this gentleman, or this lady, don't you know, Frau Hoffmann says. Before now, there was no one—no one!—who would have dared to fight me.

Not even me, her mother says and smiles.

Not even you, Frau Hoffmann says.

At the beginning of the week when she is going to die, the day after her ninetieth birthday, Frau Hoffman smiles together with her mother for the first time in her life.

There's one thing you should know, child, her mother says. You can actually put a scare into him with a handful of snow.

Really? Frau Hoffmann says, relieved.

Then she remembers it's May.

2

Oh come, dear May, and let
  The trees all bud again.
  And let us to the brook
  To see violets blow again.
  How dearly I am longing
  To see their tiny blooms
  O May, how I am longing
  To stroll about again.

They were five years old, or six, or seven when they learned this song. Now they sit here singing it with voices that have grown old, locked up in old age as if in a prison, they're still the same ones who were once five, six, and seven, but they're also irredeemably removed from this age, perhaps they won't even live to see the end of the month they're singing about, perhaps by the time the gardener is raking the autumn leaves of the trees that are just now starting to bud, they'll be lying in the ground. On Tuesday from ten to eleven, they have singing group. That's all there is on Tuesday, there's no Herr Zabel stopping by in the afternoon, and her son doesn't come either, he said he'll pick her up on Saturday and take her on an outing. What is a Tuesday? For lunch, poached eggs, and a piece of cake with whipped cream is served with the coffee, outside it begins to drizzle and keeps on into the evening. At some point Frau Hoffmann asks Sister Katrin to open the window and stays there drawing in the damp, warm air in deep breaths, it smells of leaves, just like the night she slept out in the open beside the Danube with her girlfriend. Frau Buschwitz goes to sleep with her headphones on, as she does so often.

We set out to, we'll take care of everything.

And then it all became so shabby.

We tried to take care of everything, but we went about it wrong.

If Frau Hoffmann died tonight, these would be her last words, but there wouldn't be anyone there to hear them.

On Wednesday Frau Millner says to Sister Renate at breakfast that she always eats two slices of toast. I know, Sister Renate says, loud enough for even Frau Millner, who is hard of hearing, to hear. Frau Millner says: One with jam and one with honey. I know, says Sister Renate. Her husband, though, only used to eat one. Well, if he wasn't hungrier than that, Sister Renate says. Yes, but that was a mistake, Frau Millner says, otherwise he might still be alive today. Eating keeps body and soul together, Sister Renate says. Exactly, Frau Millner says.

What is a Wednesday?

Beside Frau Millner, Frau Hoffman sits with her eyes shut, counting the seconds, because she knows that the executions start at eight o'clock. Every minute a group of ten prisoners is shot. She silently counts to ten, nodding along with the numbers, and then waits for the next minute to begin. She doesn't have to look at the clock to know when a minute is over. Finally she has grown old enough to be able to move freely in time.

One. Two. Three.

Frau Schmidt: The Russians blew up Strassmannstrasse 2 because we didn't clear away the tank barricades quickly enough. We couldn't move any faster, we were at the end of our strength.

Four. Five. Six.

Frau Podbielski: Sometimes I would mix the insides of plum pits into the dough for the honey cake, did you know you can crack open the pits of plums just like nuts?

Seven. Eight. Nine.

Frau Giesecke: When it was *subbotnik*, my children always helped gather the pieces of balled-up paper from the bushes.

The day room is full of stories not being told.

Ten.

Even during the week when Frau Hoffmann is going to die, the day after her ninetieth birthday, time is a porridge made of time, it's rubbery, refuses to pass, has to be killed, spent, served, and still keeps dragging on. What is a Thursday, a Friday? Sometimes in the afternoon this person comes by, this one or that one, and sits, and holds her hand—why?—takes her by the bony shoulder and says: Keep your chin up! Or did no one come at all? The days when someone comes and the days when she just sits there all collapse into a single day, time is a porridge made of time. Who are you? All that remains of life now is what's left at the very bottom when all the other reserves have been used up: Then the iron reserves make their appearance.

Knit one, purl one, the instructor is helping her.

I'm such an awful sheep.

But you're doing very well, Frau Hoffmann.

I never understood how it works.

Stick the needle in here and then pull the yarn through.

Oh, I see.

Bravo, Frau Hoffmann.

You know, it's not that I'm a—what's the word—a daydreamer. It's not that. It's something else: fear.

The iron reserves, fear.

Fear of doing something wrong again.

Fear of the day, fear of the night, fear of the storm and strangers coming to visit, fear of the poison in her food and the nurse who acts friendly but in truth is out to steal her gold bracelet, fear of where the wheelchair she's sitting in is being pushed, and by whom? Fear of the doctor and of the pain, fear of her son who brought her here, fear of life and fear of death, fear of all the time she still has to live through.

But Frau Hoffmann, there's nothing to be afraid of.

I have such a great fear of doing something wrong that I always do something wrong.

But look, you've already knitted an entire row perfectly, Frau Hoffmann.

No, no, something is always wrong. I know that, there's no changing it.

Here, now you turn the whole thing over and start again from the beginning.

Is this the right way?

As right as right can be.

It'll hold together?

Of course, why shouldn't it?

Approximately eighty years ago, an arts and crafts teacher in Vienna declared the work of one of her pupils *sloppy* and *shoddy*. Is it possible that this pupil was given so long a life for the sole purpose of having the sentence uttered by that loathsome Viennese woman finally canceled out, buried by a new sentence uttered by a new teacher? Has she been in the world all these many years just so these two sentences—to give just one example—can confront each other within her, and the good one defeat the bad? Might everything that's ever been said and that will be said everywhere in the world constitute a living whole, growing sometimes in one direction, sometimes in another, always balancing out in the end? So was this the end?

Knit one, purl one.

I see.

Now turn it over and start again from the beginning.

That's all there is to it?

That's all there is to it.

3

A man sits in Vienna at the Café Museum over a glass of mineral water, trying to think what he might bring back for his mother to give her pleasure, his mother who was a child in Vienna. Should he buy her a little bronze St. Stephen's Cathedral, or a real Sacher torte from Hotel Sacher, or just bring her a twig from a tree on Arenbergplatz, not far from the apartment where she used to live? He can't imagine that his mother was once a child. A year and a half ago, when he came to bring her to the Home and found her already waiting for him in her hat and coat on a chair in the vestibule, she introduced herself to him as a major in the Imperial and Royal army, ready to march off into battle. Beside her stood a small, dark-blue suitcase, and in her lap she held the little box with the gold buttons. He knew the box well, he'd used these buttons in Ufa to buy two or sometimes even three kilograms of air from his *niania*; he'd polished them when he was bored waiting for his mother, often staring at the double-headed eagle. Here in Vienna this eagle spread its wings not only atop the Hofburg, it was everywhere in the city, glancing at the same time to the right and the left: on cast-iron railings, on fountains, above the entryways to buildings, and even on the shop sign of the *Trafik* where he'd just bought himself a pack of cigarettes—and this although the Kaiser had been dead for three-quarters of a century now. Everywhere here this eagle was still spreading its wings above its two heads, as if to hold them together.

Did time in Vienna really pass so slowly?

Or not at all?

In the Eastern part of Germany, a state had been founded and had remained a state for forty years, had been a quotidian reality for forty years, with new buildings springing up, schoolchildren, the victory of Socialism, please wait to be seated, Heroes of Labor, 10-pfennig streetcar tickets, I'll petition the authorities, run down to the *Konsum* and get yourself an ice cream, Karl-Marx-Allee at the corner of Andreasstrasse, the gathering place for May 1, picking cherries in Werder, Ernst Busch singing of the Peasant's War, the lift is stuck again, Socialist sister countries, dear Comrades—and at some point, after an entire lifetime of life, everyday reality and state had broken apart, had disappeared, been stamped into the ground, wiped off the map, crumbled, been swept aside by the People— but in Vienna, it seemed to him, everything that had always been there had simply endured. Bombs falling on Vienna at the end of the war, as his mother always insisted—this is something he cannot for the life of him imagine, since all the buildings he's seen here are so vast, so unscathed.

Although he's traveled to Frankfurt am Main many times since the opening of the border, and also to London, Trieste, and once even to New York with his wife and children to see the Statue of Liberty, the man still privately thinks of Vienna as "the West." Like it or not, the scent of coffee at Café Museum reminds him of the packages his first girlfriend used to receive from her relatives in the Federal Republic; he can't stop calling the current era *Age of the Winners*, and again and again finds himself marveling at how so-called modernity appears to derive its superiority solely from the fact that it's been around for a good hundred and fifty years now. Like it or not, when he looks at the people here, he sees they are used to driving fast cars, that they know what a tax return is, and have no cause to hesitate before ordering a glass of prosecco with their breakfast. Just the way they let the door slam behind them when they walk in shows him how sure they are of being in the right world everywhere in the world. Now he too is sitting in this right world, he even has the right money in his wallet, although he's drinking water to conserve his "West money." *No dogs allowed.* The signs with the images of the dogs prohibited from entering butcher shops, restaurants and swimming pools existed in East Germany as well, and probably they existed everywhere in the world. The border that used to separate him from the West has long since fallen—but now it seems to have slipped inside him, separating the person he used to be from the one he's supposed to be now, or allowed to be. I don't know how you recognize a human being, his mother said to him last time he visited. He doesn't want prosecco with his breakfast, like it or not. And he couldn't care less if the others can tell by his way of looking around, by his hair and cheeks, that he comes from the land that has finally, rightly so, thank God, high time now, been wiped off the face of the earth, the land of—what madness—publicly owned enterprises, red carnations for your lapel on May 1, rigged elections, old men wearing berets left over from the Spanish Civil War, and dialectics taught at school. *A Man—how proud that sounds.* Getting off the night train at six in the morning, he saw people sleeping on pieces of cardboard in the station. In what world had he spent the last forty years? What happened to that world? Will he have the heart of a dog now for the rest of his life?

Later he leaves the café in his own company, meaning to stroll for a little while before his appointment that isn't until the afternoon, they're selling horse meat at the Naschmarkt, herbs, apples, and flowers; he promenades across the square then strolls across to the Rechte Wienzeile; it's still too early in the day for the porn cinema there, he has no desire to desire anything, blindly he strolls down a side street, makes a right turn without a plan, and onward:

streetcar tracks, the entryways of the buildings giving off a smell of quicklime and dust as though it were summer already, he passes grimy shop windows, walking ever farther down this street. He's happy not to have to go look at anything a foreigner in Vienna is supposed to see, he likes walking like this through everyday reality. In a spot where a very long time ago an angel kept watch over a building's front entrance, the low building no longer stands, instead there's a modern five-story hotel. Indeed, the building where his great-grandmother once lived fell victim to one of the few bombs dropped in the final days of the war, in March 1945, but by then his great-grandmother had already been dead for more than four years, her apartment had been emptied out and passed on to others. But he knows neither who his great-grandmother was, nor where she lived, he steps to one side when the revolving door deposits a group of tourists onto the sidewalk. As far as this descendent of a Viennese resident is concerned, Vienna has been washed clean of stories, it took less than a human lifetime for the city to lose all connection to him. Less than a human lifetime for homeland and origins to diverge. He is free, doubly free; he carries around within him a vast dark land: all the stories his mother never told him or that she hid from him; perhaps he carries with him even those stories his mother never knew or heard of, he can't get rid of them, but he can't lose them either, since he doesn't even know them, since all of this lies buried deep within him; for when he slipped from his mother's womb, he was already filled with interior spaces that didn't belong to him, and he can't just look inside to inspect his own interior. His father once spent three weeks in Berlin almost forty years ago, but he didn't know about it, how could he have? His father later spent an eternity living in Vorkuta, and twelve years ago he died there, but the son knows neither of these things. The son can make his home anywhere in the world, in Berlin for example. If he knew what questions to ask, knew what, where, and to whom, then an official of the Jewish Community of

Vienna would surely be able to dig up one or the other list and inform him that his great-grandmother was brought to Opole in the district of Lublin with the first transport of February '41, that his grandmother moved six times within Vienna and then was sent via Minsk to Maly Trostenets in July '42, and that his aunt spent many months hiding in a friend's apartment and then was sent in '44 to Auschwitz. But given what he knows, he finds Vienna just as dusty as any other metropolis. Kettenbrückengasse, Mariahilfer Strasse, Siebensterngasse, Mondscheingasse. There on the *otherer* side, as his mother would say, is a second-hand shop; who knows, maybe he'll find something here that he can bring her.

The miniature grandfather clock, standing on a shelf beside the entryway, is just striking ten with tinny strokes, although he knows it has to be at least 11:30 by now. All around he sees tables and cabinets, chairs with woven seats, stools and ottomans, glass cases with jewelry tangled in old silverware; lamps dangle from the ceiling, and the walls are hung with oil paintings, mirrors, barometers, crucifixes, and trays that once held movable type; shelves bear candelabras, plates, books, and glasses, and under the tables are wooden buckets and baskets filled with linens. Everything is squeezed in tightly together, each object casting its shadow on the next, so that, even on this bright May day, the room lies in its own twilight. At first the man cannot make out a seller, and no one speaks to him in greeting; only after his eyes have become accustomed to the low light does he see a man sitting in an armchair off in the back, immersed in a book.

What might please his mother? His mother who didn't want to take anything when she moved to the rest home but the yellow wall hanging with its Uzbek sun, the small dark-blue suitcase, whose contents are unknown to him, and the little box with the gold buttons. He wouldn't mind acquiring this set of Goethe's writings for his own use—the final authorized edition, surprisingly complete with all its volumes—that no doubt costs less here than at an antiquarian bookshop. At random he pulls out Volume 9, the spine of which is a bit scraped, and leafs through it; he reads "Farewell," then puts the book back in its place. How can he carry an entire Goethe edition on the train to Berlin? A brooch set with amethysts might be nice, or a silver spoon with the Vienna city arms, but he doesn't feel like asking the shopkeeper to open the glass case. Finally he sees a miniature double portrait leaning up against a Meissen soup tureen, a double portrait of Prussian Kaiser Wilhelm II and Kaiser Franz Joseph as allies, *In Steadfast Loyalty* is written on the picture, and since his Viennese mother has wound up in Prussia, he thinks it might work, the piece's political context now lying far in the past; he takes the picture from the shelf, approaches the man and asks: Excuse me, how much?

4

The owner of the Goethe edition and the clock is already nearly eighty when she has to leave everything behind, and in February '41, leaning on her cousin's arm, she begins her journey to the Jewish Home for the Aged on Malzgasse, which, for the sake of convenience, has been designated the first collection point for deportations to the East. The clock strikes eleven, the clock strikes twelve, *Morning wind wings about the shady bay*, then her cousin returns to the empty apartment. He sits for a while at the table, where a moment ago he shared a last cup of tea with the old woman. *Es vert mir finster in di oygn,* everything's going black before my eyes. Then the clock strikes one. The old woman was forced to turn in her seven-armed candelabra the year before, for the metal collection. It's surely long since been melted down. But the Goethe edition at least: the man now packs it up, grabbing three or four volumes at a time, in the very suitcase in which he transported it twenty years before on his cart. He removes the pendulum from the clock, wrapping the clock in a pillowcase and tying it up to make a package that he can put in a coal sack and hang over his shoulder. With suitcase and sack he leaves the apartment, which has grown completely cold, a thin sheet of ice has already formed on top of the water in the bucket. If he hadn't slipped the clock's pendulum into the breast pocket of his jacket, he'd think he was still hearing the clock ticking right through the sack and the soft fabric, as though he were hearing it through snow, he could swear the clock's hands were still moving behind his back. After all, before the old lady started on her journey to Malzgasse, she had wound the clock one last time, just as she had done every morning for the last fifty years. With the stopped clock on his back, the old woman's cousin walks through the February cold, the pendulum peeking out of his breast pocket with its delicate little hook, and the key to wind it is in his trouser pocket, where it is slowly growing warm. The cousin walks to the neighborhood around Arenberg-platz, rings a doorbell, speaks with someone, nods, then takes the streetcar to Mariahilfer Strasse 117, rings the bell, speaks, nods, then heads to Linzer Strasse 439, rings, speaks; Haidgasse 4, and finally he finds himself standing on Dampfschiffstrasse 10/6 in District II before a door, he rings the bell, speaks, and here he is finally relieved of his burden that has now become an inheritance, a reminder to the woman answering of something she doesn't want to be reminded of, objects speak without speaking, and the woman now knows something she didn't want to know: that there is a moment when it is forever too late. Last of all, the now-warm key from the cousin's trouser pocket—oh, right—and the pendulum. The woman takes the key, pendulum, suitcase, and the coal sack, and carries them to a room belonging to her only in part, strangers are sitting there on beds, strange children playing under the table, strangers quarreling, and here—as if all these things had nothing to do with her—she takes the packet out of the sack, unwraps it, places the clock on the table, hooks the pendulum in its place, and already the clockwork begins ticking again, her mother's life is still there in the tightly wound spring; she shoos a few children away, sits down in front of the clock, and watches as time—which is now forever too late—passes. Time is like a briar that has gotten caught in wool, you tear it out with all your strength and throw it over your shoulder. Minutes pass that no longer matter, cleanly divided by the minute hand one from the next.

Yet again, the suitcase and coal sack with the clock wrapped in its pillowcase are transported by the woman through the streets of Vienna, for a new official directive has ordered her to move from Dampfschiffstrasse to Obere Donaustrasse, and three months later from Obere Donaustrasse to Hammer-Purgstall-Gasse 3/12. Although the woman finds these moves quite burdensome, she nonetheless lugs the *Complete Works* of Goethe along with her, as well as the clock, these last two remaining possessions of her mother, who has long since been deported. And when she arrives at one or the other location, she unwraps the clock, winds it, then lays the key beside it, just as her mother always used to. Perhaps there's secretly something magical about these inherited belongings, just like in the fairy tale, where, in time of need, a comb thrown over your shoulder can grow into a forest.

But no forest has grown as of August 13, 1942, when she boards the train at the Aspang Station in Vienna that will take her to Minsk. Forcing the doors, clearing out the shared apartment that served as a transit station for Jews at Hammer-Purgstall-Gasse 3/12, and making an inventory takes the Gestapo's Division for the Processing of Jewish Personal Effects two and a half days. The clock has meanwhile come to a stop. The key for winding it lies, as always, beside it. Chaim Safir sticks the key through the little oval opening, through which you can see the pendulum, and into the clock case, then he puts the clock in a laundry basket, in which a stack of plates, a vase made of porcelain, several glasses and a crystal carafe are already awaiting deportation. To keep things from breaking, Chaim Safir stuffs some items of clothing between them, then he picks up the basket, carries it downstairs, and says to Herr Gschwandtner: All that's left now is the furniture. Herr Gschwandtner follows him to do a check, looking around the room, he opens the cabinet doors, looks under the beds, pushes a little footstool aside, deftly pulling the suitcase out from behind it, saying: It's probably full of jewels, you idiot. Chaim Safir says: I'm sorry, I overlooked the suitcase. Herr Gschwandtner says, The thing weighs a ton. At first the lid refuses to open, but then it does, such a *mazl*, Herr Gschwandtner says to Chaim Safir, nothing but books, just look what's on the back of them: nothing but Goethe; he slams the suitcase shut again. *To be or not to be*, he says, grinning, as he gets to his feet. Chaim Safir nods without meeting Herr Gschwandtner's eyes. Herr Gschwandtner pokes at the suitcase with his shoe-tip and says: This one goes downstairs too.

Suitcase and clock spend the weekend in the depot along with all the other items. On Monday morning the assessor comes and sorts the new arrivals according to value: the basket with the clock, carafe, and dishes is sent to Krummbaumgasse, ground floor, for private sale; since the suitcase looks so shabby, he doesn't even open it before saying: That too. On the ground floor of Krummbaumgasse, shabby suitcases like this one—packed and then abandoned—sell for 2 *reichsmark* a piece (a pig in a poke, you take your chances, part and parcel, lock, stock, and barrel, blind man's bluff, who doesn't like a surprise), each is sold along with its contents, but opening the lid beforehand is not allowed. The newspaper prints a notice announcing the arrival of a new assortment of furniture and accessories for sale; a young wartime bride applies for an invitation to view the goods, enclosing her pay slip, she's certainly poor enough and has a husband on the Eastern front, making ends meet isn't easy for her. If she receives an invitation, she'll be allowed to bring two friends or relatives when she comes, and she does receive one, so she brings her mother and a girlfriend—oh just look at that, isn't that adorable, and really it's not expensive. A vase, a carafe made of crystal, a set of sheets, or a plate. Just look at the clock, you can see its pendulum through the hole, maybe it doesn't work, oh I'm sure it does, what's that rattling around inside?, look, the key, I'll fish it out, careful, let's wind it up, my goodness, look at the size of this platter, why are you surprised? they're the ones who carve up babies, what nonsense, it's really beautiful, and I'm going to take this suitcase, it's such a good deal, go ahead, who knows what's inside, Jesus it's heavy, maybe stones, maybe treasure, could I possibly have just a tiny peek inside first? Madame, a peek would cost more, all right, if you insist, how bad can it be, I'll take it as is, maybe it'll be the surprise of my life, but let's not open it till we get home, why not? I want to see what's inside, why do you always have to be so impatient.... The clock strikes three, even though it's only just after nine-thirty. What a pretty chime, I wouldn't like it myself, it sounds annoying, not to me, I'll fix it to show the right time, I think it's pretty, so do I, what do you want with a clock?, everyone needs a clock. And I'll take the platter. The Jewish platter? Why not? I'll baptize it this Saturday: I'm making ham hocks.

Two years later when the war finally comes to an end, the wartime bride has a daughter, but her husband fell in Russia. The miniature grandfather clock strikes with tinny strokes all the hours that a life contains in peacetime, it strikes from one to twelve, one to twelve, and the next day the same thing, twice from one to twelve, it strikes at the crack of dawn when the janitor's broom bumps against the front door from the outside, it strikes in the empty apartment all morning long while the girl is at school and the woman is at her office, strikes in the afternoon during the hour for coffee and cake, and in the evening during the lullaby *The moon is arisen*, it even strikes late at night when the war widow lets down her hair without a man to hang his belt over the back of the chair. It strikes from one to twelve for all the length of a peaceful Aryan life.

When the war widow approaches her fiftieth birthday, her elderly mother dies, and she dissolves her mother's household with her daughter, who is meanwhile grown; in the basement, she finds the old Goethe edition: the surprise of her life back then, the pig in the poke; the volumes smell of the cellar but are not mildewed. The man in the antique shop next door, who's always sitting around reading, pays her a respectable sum for the *bit of rubbish*. The shabby valise that in its day cost her mother a mere 2 *reichsmark*, even full, also contains an assortment of patches in different colors, and these she might still have use for herself.

For over twenty years more, this clock goes on striking its tinny hours in this chance Vienna household, each day from one to twelve and then again, until day after day comes to an end; her daughter has her own life now, and when her grandchildren come to visit, they peer through the oval hole to see the clock's pendulum swing back and forth without ever getting tired, but they aren't allowed to touch, the clock needs dusting, the woman already needs reading glasses, and walking is starting to be difficult for her; her daughter visits far too seldom, alas, but what can you do? The woman sometimes falls asleep in front of the television, not waking up until the clock strikes twelve in the middle of the night; her grandchildren are fairly spoiled; the woman eats a crescent-shaped *Kipferl* for breakfast each morning; she goes on living and living and winding the clock, always placing the key beside it. And finally, when her final hour has tolled, the woman dies a peaceful Aryan death.

Her daughter doesn't like all the old clutter one bit; an apartment should be empty and bright, and she already has more than enough in her own household; good Lord, all the things her mother kept squirreled away: the shabby valise with the patches is the first to go, and as for the rest—just look, that same old antique shop dealer is still sitting right there in his shop reading! Might he have use for a clock, really a very special piece from Grandmother's era? Yes, the key is still there, and when the clock strikes the hour, it has such a bright, friendly chime it really warms the heart to hear it.

5

The salesman glances up from his book only briefly, 280 shillings, he says, and goes on reading. And so the man buys his mother the miniature *In Steadfast Loyalty* as a souvenir from Vienna, and since the time he's spent in the shop, though considerable, is less than an hour, he doesn't hear the next striking of the miniature grandfather clock that displayed the wrong time when he entered. On his trip back to Berlin, he thinks briefly of the Goethe edition—there's an empty couchette on the night train where he might have stowed it—but the spine of Volume 9 was damaged, and besides, who knows whether he'd still have time to read an edition of collected works, he isn't getting any younger.

6

Saturday is Frau Hoffmann's ninetieth birthday. Her place at the table between Frau Millner and Frau Schröder is set with a bouquet of flowers from the Home's administration and a little bottle of sparkling wine. When she sits down, all those who are still in a position to sing begin singing when Sister Renate gives the signal: *How glad we are that you were born, your bir-ir-irthday is today.* Frau Hoffmann takes note of the fact that it's her birthday and thanks everyone. Frau Millner nods to her, or maybe she's just nodding because her toast with honey tastes so good, while Frau Schröder is concentrating exclusively on not spilling her coffee. On the way back to her room, Sister Renate says: Today your son's coming to take you on an outing, isn't that right, Frau Hoffmann? Oh, I didn't realize that, Frau Hoffmann says. But then before her son arrives she wants to comb her hair and wipe the jam stain off her jacket. But even just raising her arm to the level of her head is difficult for her, my own body is already too large for me, she says to Sister Renate; don't worry, the nurse says, I'll pretty you up, she takes the comb from Frau Hoffmann's hand, draws it a couple of times through her sparse gray hair saying, at eleven I'll come back and bring you downstairs, all right? Sure, Frau Hoffman says, I'm sure that will be fine.

And then she is sitting beside her son in who knows what sunshine, beneath who knows what blue sky with plenty of good fresh air, in the middle of the world.

It's so wonderful you're here, she says.

I'm glad to see you, too.

It's such a great help to me, but you don't know anything about it, and it's good you don't know, it isn't good to know more.

Her son is silent.

Tell me, was your trip nice?

Her son tells her about Vienna, the Naschmarkt and Café Museum.

I have such a longing.

Her son says: I brought you something.

Pretty, she says, inspecting Kaiser William II and Kaiser Franz Joseph.

It's from a shop on Mondscheingasse, do you know it?

You know, I want to live and I cannot. When I die, a place will be empty, that's all, and a new place will be occupied.

I love you, her son says, taking his mother's hand,

Really? That's nice, she says.

Her hand lies cold and bony in his large, warm hand.

You know, she says, I am afraid that everything will be lost—
that *the trace* will be lost.

What trace? her son asks.

I don't know anymore: from where or to where.

Her son is silent.

A few clouds are crossing the broad sky. Two airplanes flying
high in the air have made trails up there that are gradually turning
back into sky. The son recalls that until only a few years ago there
would sometimes be an earsplitting crack in the middle of a silence
like this when supersonic aircraft broke the sound barrier during a
military maneuver. Now the Russians—generally referred to as *our
friends*—have long since gone home, and the training grounds of
the National People's Army have been relocated; and probably it
is no longer legal to break through the sound barrier just as part of
some drill. Now everything is quiet, and the sky is almost as empty
as it was in the age of the hunter-gatherers.

I think that if we try playing, it will be a peculiar sort of game,
his mother says.

Four weeks before the Berlin Wall fell, his mother received the
National Prize First Class for her life's work. She walked to the front
of the auditorium on his arm to receive the certificate and the little
box. Now he is sitting with her on a bench at the edge of the woods,
the leaves rustle behind them, and before them lies a wide, gently
sloping field, upon which the blue-green wheat is still only knee
high. When the wind sweeps across it, it looks almost like water.

I just wanted to tell you, his mother says, this is my good, good
lovely farewell.

Oh, mother, he says, stroking her back.

My fear of the future, she says, has not yet failed.

A couple of his mother's friends wanted to come to celebrate her birthday, but he told them no. Because he was ashamed for his mother? Or because he was of the opinion that his mother should be preserved in her friends' memories just as she used to be? Whom was he doing a favor: her, her friends, or himself?

It sinks down over you from above to below—you don't know what side it's coming from. I don't know, and you probably don't know either.

No, I don't know.

Never has he known as little as he does now. The only thing he knows is that his not-knowing is of a very different sort than hers. His mother's not-knowing is as deep as a river on whose distant shore there must be a very different sort of world than the one he lives in.

I don't know how you recognize a human being.

I don't know from whom I can demand everything.

Do they come to us or from us?

I don't know what is coming.

I don't know anything.

I don't know when big is. When is little?

I don't know what to do.

I don't know where I was at home.

There is so much I don't know.

I don't know what is happening.

It begins slowly, and then it ends slowly. I don't know which I like better.

I don't know if my heart will beat again.

I don't know the big difference.

I don't know.

I don't know and I don't understand either.

I know what I know—but it isn't all tied up with names.

I think this is all make-believe.

I think that's it.

In this land to which his mother is crossing over, no longer able to understand anything she once understood, she will no longer need any words, this much he understands. For one brief, sharp, clear moment, he understands what it would be like if he could arrive there along with her: The wheat field would be there right from the start, just like the rustling of the leaves at his back, the silence would be filled to the brim—that deafening crack living only in his memory, absent now—and the memory that filled out this silence would be just as real as the footsteps of all the human beings walking upon the earth at this moment, along with their falling down, their jumping, crawling, and sleeping at this very moment, just as real as all that mutely lay or flowed within the earth: the springs, the roots, and the dead; the cry of the cuckoo off to one side would be just as real as the stones crunching beneath the sole of his shoe, as the coolness of the evening and the light falling through the leaves to the ground before him, as his hand that he is using to stroke his mother's back, feeling her bones beneath her thin, old skin, bones that will soon be laid bare—briefly, sharply, clearly, he knows for one instant what it would feel like if the audible and the inaudible, things distant and near, the inner and outer, the dead and the living were simultaneously there, nothing would be above anything else, and this moment when everything was simultaneously there would last forever. But because he is a human being—a middle-aged man, with a wife, two children, a profession—because he still has some time ahead of him, time during which he can look up something he doesn't know in an encyclopedia or ask one of his colleagues, this knowing free of language passes from him just as suddenly as it arrived. He'll be prevented from seeing this other world with the eyes of his mother for a good earthly time, by the absence of the most crucial thing: the going away.

I dreamed that I was dreaming.

And suddenly it was no longer a dream.

7

Frau Buschwitz is already asleep when the son brings his mother back to her room that evening. On the table at his mother's bedside is a rinsed-out glass soda bottle with modeling clay stuck to it. The clay has been shaped into a red "90," surrounded by a yellow ring, outside the ring are sausage-shaped green and blue rays. The bottle holds a single rose, and leaning up against it is a birthday card with the words *Happy Birthday!—from Herr Zander and his wife*. Who are Herr Zander and his wife? her son asks. Good friends, his mother replies. Aha, her son says. Before he leaves, he takes the miniature and leans it against the bottle, too. *In Steadfast Loyalty*.

Lately, his mother says, I find myself wanting to address the burden with its proper title, the burden title.

Will you be all right? her son asks.

Oh yes, his mother says. I forced a century to its arms. For the moment, I mean.

I'll let the nurse know it's time to help you change and go to bed, all right?

I don't know, his mother says, what it can mean that we are so sad.

I'll be going then, Mother, her son says.

Of course, Son, his mother says, go ahead, and put your hat on.

At 52.58867 degrees latitude north, 13.39529 degrees longitude east.

When the phone rings at six in the morning, the son knows it can only be for him. Between four and five in the morning, unfortunately, it must be so difficult for him, but perhaps better this way for his mother, all of us in the hand of God.

For one week more he will awaken every morning at precisely 4:17 a.m., every morning, precisely at the moment of the greatest silence, just before the birds begin to sing. For the first time in his life, he will have dreams during these nights that he still remembers when he wakes up.

His mother is lying there just barely underground, her head is still sticking out: Are you the one who was with me in Ufa, she asks. Yes, he answers and lifts up the ten centimeters of earth like a blanket to place a photograph of his two children upon her breast.

And then he wakes up, it's perfectly quiet, and then all at once the birds begin to sing, it is 4:17 a.m.

Many mornings he will get up at this early hour that belongs only to him and go into the kitchen, and there he will weep bitterly as he has never wept before, and still, as his nose runs and he swallows his own tears, he will ask himself whether these strange sounds and spasms are really all that humankind has been given to mourn with.

ACKNOWLEDGMENTS

For their support of my work, I would like to thank Wolf-Erich Eckstein from the Archives of the Israelitische Kultusgemeinde Vienna, the Vienna Stadt- und Landesarchiv, the Archives of the Akademie der Künste Berlin, the Deutsches Rundfunkarchiv and "Haus Immanuel" in Berlin-Niederschönhausen.

JE

And for their help with the translation, thanks are due also to Sebastian Schulman, Rose Waldman, Zackary Sholem Berger, Gal Kober, Tali Konas, Philippe Roth, Edoardo Ballerini, as well as to Richard Gehr, Amanda Hong, Helen Graves, and my valiant editor Declan Spring.

SB

JENNY ERPENBECK was born in East Berlin in 1967. New Directions publishes her books *The Old Child & Other Stories*, *The Book of Words*, and *Visitation*, which National Public Radio called "a story of the century as seen through the objects we've known and lost along the way."

The translator of Hermann Hesse, Franz Kafka, Yoko Tawada, and Robert Walser, **SUSAN BERNOFSKY** is currently working on a biography of Robert Walser.